THE URCHIN OF WALTON HALL

Emma Hardwick

COPYRIGHT

Title: THE URCHIN OF WALTON HALL

Paperback published in 2021

Copyright © 2021 Emma Hardwick

ISBN: 9798631840409

BOOK CARD

Other books by Emma Hardwick

Forging the Shilling Girl

The Sailor's Lost Daughters

The Scullery Maid's Salvation

The Widow of the Valley

The Christmas Songbird

The Slum Lady

The Vicar's Wife

The Lost Girl's Beacon of Hope

CONTENTS

1

THE TRAVELLING SALESMAN

Birdsong and sunshine were in the midday air as Mr McAlister angrily paced up the drive of Walton Hall, with as much dogged determination as a soldier capturing a military objective. Reaching the butter-coloured stone portico, standing on the grey porch flagstones, he put down his brown leather briefcase. He carefully leaned his walking cane next to the glossy black door.

With a deep breath, he composed himself as he made sure his collar was flat, his tie was straight, and his coat was smooth. He had one shot at this encounter.

He stretched out a thin, pale finger, rang the doorbell and then waited, staring blankly at the door.

Momentarily, a servant opened it.

"Good morning, Sir. May I 'elp you?"

"Yes, I think you can," he replied.

With a visitor being a rare occurrence, the lady of the house, the curious Mrs Harvey, glided into the nearby hallway. She peered at the entrance as Meg stepped aside a little, to avoid obscuring her view.

"I'm looking for the man of the house, a Mr Harvey," explained the man.

"Of course. Fetch Mr Harvey, Meg."

With a thin, unconvincing smile, she studied the gentleman in the doorway.

"He will be with you presently, Sir."

Hannah Harvey knew his face from somewhere, but where—? *That's it. He's from the church congregation at the Sunday morning service, although not regularly.*

Never one to see the good in a person, she decided the fellow was some kind of knave knocking on their door with an artful scheme to sell them something dubious to make ends meet. The briefcase must contain some sales materials or samples, no doubt.

With Meg's knock at the study door, Robert Harvey raised his head from the pile of papers spread out on his walnut desk, for the first time in quite some hours.

"A visitor, Sir. Out front. Wants to see you, if you please."

"Thank you, Meg."

His voice trailed off as he walked downstairs. Seeing the man at the entrance, he stiffened and stood firm at the threshold, his snooping wife standing a couple of paces behind.

With growing suspicion, Mrs Harvey slid her head round the neighbouring parlour door.

"Children, go and play in the back courtyard—now!"

Obediently, they fled in single-file, fearing another out-burst of their mother's fiery temper.

Without saying a word, the smartly dressed visitor punched Robert Harvey cleanly in the face. It was a solid right hook and would have surely made the visitor's hand ring out in pain, had the anger not numbed it so.

Mrs Harvey saw her husband lose his footing and fall back against the open door, clearly in shock. His left hand hunted instinctively for the handle to steady himself, desperately trying to minimise any sign of weakness or shame. Dazed and speechless by the agony he felt in his jaw, coupled with the metallic taste of blood in his mouth, he glared at McAlister.

The visitor yelled:

"You stay away from my wife, Harvey. I know exactly what you're up to. Taking her for yourself while I'm away on business, that's what."

He lunged, pushed Mr Harvey's shoulder against the door with his left hand. Then, with his right, McAlister punched him in the stomach with such ferocity that Robert Harvey doubled up in pain, then collapsed.

"That's just so you know who's in charge, Sir. You stay away from her—Understand?"

Mrs Harvey looked down towards the carpet and her husband sprawled upon it. She took control and shooed a cowering Meg away with her hand.

"For God's sake, go, woman. There is nothing to gawp at."

A wheezing Mr Harvey found his feet and bellowed:

"Get off my property. Now! You, Sir, are a liar. You will not come to my house and besmirch my good name, nor upset my family with your accusations, nor attack me with your wayward fists ever again. Do you hear me?"

"That all depends on whether you lie with my wife again, Mr Harvey," was the mocking reply. "I will come back with a weapon next time. Do you hear me?"

"Stay away," snarled Robert; teeth bared like an angry guard dog.

Mr McAlister picked up his briefcase and his stick which had fallen on the floor in the skirmish, warning:

"I've got the measure of you, my man."

He turned on his heels and marched purposefully along the driveway and disappeared through the gate. He headed left to take the lane which led towards the nearby market town of Woodborough.

Without a word, Mr Harvey closed the door and returned to the study, giving no explanation; not that his wife seemed to need one.

Mrs Harvey sat alone in the parlour, simmering, reflecting on the news of her husband's adultery.

After an hour of frustrating jabbing at her embroidery, the wooden ring clattered on the table as she left to discuss the matter with her husband.

She entered the study, closed the door behind her, in an attempt to shield her children from the truth, then began to lay down the law.

"I'm sure I don't need to remind you, Robert, that it is my family's money that bought this house. The initial investment my father made in your business has made you the man you are today, and you owe me loyalty for that."

"McAlister is a lunatic, Hannah. He has clearly mistaken me for some other philandering fool. If he's not there, how can he know for sure it is me? He's a liar and a braggart—causing a scene to tarnish my reputation like that. What's next with the fellow?

Blackmail? I should inform the police about the menace."

Hannah glared at him.

"Do you really think I am that stupid, Robert? How often have you tried to hide your frequent, unexplained absences of late? To be blunt, I have lost count. You do realise your shameful conduct will alienate us further from my family. There will be no more funds forthcoming to support your money pit of a business. What then?"

Robert became defensive.

"Am I to believe that you (and your beloved family) will believe a stranger's unsolicited, poisonous words over your husband's own?"

The angry delivery of his comeback caused his split lip to crack open again. Blood was collecting in the grooves of his teeth. He sucked it away, running his tongue behind his lips and swallowing hard.

Being hen-pecked in his own house was something he simply would not tolerate.

"I had planned to stay at home with you and the children this afternoon, Hannah, but under the circumstances, I've changed my mind. I have no interest in hearing any more of your lecturing today."

He brushed past her with his papers, bundling them in his case. Of late, crises were at every turn for Robert Harvey. Bad news flowed from his colliery far more freely than the coal these days. Discontent simmered amongst his workers. Their living conditions were squalid; the sanitary conditions of some of the housing was the worst in the area. Cases of black lung were on the rise, robbing good dependable men from their families, and the workplace. Finding new seams to mine on his land had proved fraught with danger and difficulty, with mineshafts over 500 feet deep becoming the norm. One of the older shafts had recently collapsed and another, reaching out dangerously beneath a lake had flooded—thankfully not killing anyone yet—but it was only a matter of time before the devil struck someone down in the darkness.

There had been some initial investment in the mining venture, but regrettably, not where it was most needed, mainly frittered away on structures and facilities above ground, rather than better methods of extraction. Robert's string of poor decisions had left little money for the materials needed to expand and shore up new profitable mine shafts. Clearing the collapsed and flooded areas at great expense depleted their coffers further. Recent changes to the law prohibiting the use of child labour had proved cripplingly expensive. Robert Harvey's coal reserves were fighting tooth and nail not to be liberated from their underground hiding place.

Orders were withering away faster than he could secure them. Poor prioritisation had led to trouble meeting the demands of valuable long-standing customers. The penalties for contractual breaches, and cancellations of future business in preference to a more reputable supplier, meant his colliery's finances were in a perilous state.

Robert Harvey had very little idea how he would solve this perfect storm of pit problems. In comparison, appeasing Hannah over a secret dalliance with another man's wife was not his priority.

He announced in the parlour:

"I am leaving for the colliery. I will not be back for quite some time. Do not wait up."

And with that, he was gone.

Given the current production problems and rising worker discontent, he was not looking forward to being at on-site, but it was still preferable to being at home. He settled into perusing his papers which proved to be a useful distraction.

Nigh on midnight, he returned to Walton Hall, feeling strained and tired.

In the parlour, he poured a large measure of whiskey, quaffing it in one go, then poured out another one, slightly bigger.

There was a timid knock at the door, which was obviously not his angry wife's. The door barely opened, and a soft voice floated in:

"A bowl of soup to warm your tired bones, Sir?"

"Thank you, Meg. That would be most agreeable."

After setting it down, Meg left the room. A few mouthfuls later, he pushed the bowl away, deciding his appetite had abandoned him too. It would be a night where he preferred the burn of spirits to hot soup.

Needing a brief respite from his woes, he opted not to return to the colliery at dawn. An early start would achieve a lot less than a good night's rest to quieten his troubled mind. He also needed some space to formulate a new plan. None of the current ones had seemed to work. *I'll return with a fresh eye at lunchtime.*

He drank another whiskey then braved going upstairs to his bedroom and his enraged wife. *Please let her be asleep.*

2

LIGHTNING DOES STRIKE TWICE

The next day, the sun tried to show its face on that very gloomy morning, but it could not make its way through the dark clouds. The sky's grey-blackness hung heavy behind the matching lead-covered church spire in the distance. The threat of rain was not far away.

The vicar of Woodborough, Howard Swinnerton, had decided to busy himself with some pressing loose ends inside St Mary's Church. *Let's hope the clouds blow over, and I can avoid a soaking walking back to the vicarage.*

He began by changing the order of service notice in the porch, humming a hymn to himself, taking his time to line up the pinned paper neatly within the display panel. A silvery-white flash of lightning and the instantaneous loud grumble of thunder broke his concentration. Gazing through the stone porch archway, he was met with the appearance of stair-rod rain. Looking more carefully, he could also discern the shape of two people, a mother and a child, sheltering under the lichgate. He swung the glass door closed.

The two figures were dressed in rags, the wind flapping the fabric like a tattered flag on a pole. He believed them not to be his parishioners, but as a man of God, he felt obliged to see if they required assistance in the awful weather.

He reached inside the church, grabbed his wide-brimmed hat from the peg, then his thick woollen coat, wrapping it around him tightly, and left the porch.

"Good morning, Madam. It seems quite a cold day to be out without a coat. Are you all right?"

"Yes—and no, vicar."

He raised his eyebrows to encourage her to explain further.

The beleaguered young woman and her child looked destitute; their faces were grubby with dirt, their beauty faded by the hardship of the daily grind of poverty. The mother's fingernails surely had enough soil under them to set potatoes. *Maybe, she has just left the workhouse or could she perhaps be on her way there?*

"I need some 'elp, vicar."

He braced himself for the customary request of a shilling from the parish funds—to 'tide them over'.

"Please continue."

"I'm looking for Walton 'all, your worship. It's meant to be around these parts."

"Indeed, it is, Madam."

He looked down at the young girl beside the woman, her head tipped right back so she could beam up at him, her face partially covered with tresses of wet, wayward hair. He guessed she was about ten years old.

"Yes. The 'arvey's live there. Them's that own the colliery."

"May I ask why you need to see them? Is your visit business or personal?"

"My father works—worked," she corrected herself, "—as a shepherd on the land near the colliery. 'e rented a small cottage up there where we all lived."

"I am not sure I see your point, Madam? Is your visit to do with renting the cottage?"

"I ain't going back there, even if I could. No, my visit is very much a personal one. 'Appy? I don't mean no bother."

"Very well. I shall escort you myself."

He could see the woman was clearly down on her luck and in need of some assistance. Whether the help was deserved or not remained to be seen. He also wanted to police her visit, not trusting her motive to be an honourable one. One thing was clear, she had a terrible cough and standing here debating in the storm was clearly in no-one's interest. *She will surely catch her death in this weather, and where would that leave that poor child?*

Perhaps she's really a widowed labourer's wife. The men's wages are abysmal. Living from hand to mouth is as good as it gets for those folks. There are never any savings, except a crust of bread tucked under a pillow if a family was lucky.

If she was looking to get money from the Harveys, Howard Swinnerton did not share her optimism. There had been meagre contributions to the collection plate from them after his church services for some months. Some of the less charitable Woodborough shopkeepers gossiped about larger orders being placed on 'tick'.

"The weather is atrocious; I shall see you get there promptly."

They made their way up the storm-battered Church Lane and onto the High Street. The vicar walked a pace ahead, trying to lead them and shield them from the worst of the weather at the same time, a fruitless exercise. Their dark, dirty and tattered clothes were cut right through by the wind and soaked by the downpour.

Presently, they were at Walton Hall, all sheltering under the portico.

The vicar reached out and rang the doorbell. Meg's face appeared from behind the heavy door as it creaked open.

"Good morning, vicar. What brings you here?"

The woman crept in front of the holy man and beamed. Having an inkling what the visit might be about after the surprise kerfuffle on the doorstep yesterday, Meg suggested:

"Shall I get the man of the house, for you?"

"Yes—Let's not trouble, Mrs Harvey," advised Reverend Swinnerton.

We don't need any more help around the household. This visit can only mean one thing, surely?

After a short wait, the vicar saw Mr Harvey appear at the door. He seemed to be studying the woman's face, trying to make sense of the situation.

The sight of the small cut on his lip surprised the vicar; and if he wasn't mistaken, a bruise was forming on Robert's cheek too? Noticing he was under scrutiny, Mr Harvey took a short pace backwards, shielding his face in a light veil of darkness, and stood just inside the doorway.

It surprised the vicar to pick up so clearly on Mr Harvey's bristling. *Was it disapproval for the unexpected interruption? Or something else?* Whatever it was, the head of Walton Hall was clearly not pleased to see the woman.

"She asked to see you, Sir, on a personal matter, so, I brought them here myself. I didn't want them wandering the lanes catching their deaths. I hope you don't mind. I thought it might be something to do with the young labourers at the colliery. She's not really told me a great deal—"

He trailed off, sensing Harvey's rage building. *Oh no. It's her.*

The woman looked Robert plainly in the eye, trying to stifle her coughing and wheezing.

"I've been ill for quite some time, Sir. And as my dear old shepherd father died of cold out in the fields last week, on them 'ills right by your colliery—"

"What's that got to do with me, Madam? I run the mine, not the outlying land." he interrupted with impatience.

"I can no longer support myself, Sir. I know I am workhouse-bound. Done for. No money. No relatives. Nuffin."

"And—?"

"There is no one to care for the child."

As they had been talking, the young girl had made her way in front of her mother to try to escape the storm. A deafening rumble of thunder was accompanied by a vicious wind, an almighty gust. It blew the young girl's mess of loose hair away from her face. Underneath the dirt, Robert Harvey could make out a distinct likeness in her features. So too, could the vicar.

"She's your child. You know she is. You can see the resemblance, Sir, surely you can? There is no denying it. Do the right thing by your child, for I can no longer look after 'er, or myself. I cannot see 'er in the workhouse though, when there is a chance I can save 'er, if not me."

Robert Harvey took a deep breath and assessed the situation. *Was this divine retribution for all those carnal sins I've committed with reckless abandon? Perhaps it was time to atone before matters get any worse.*

Of late, keeping his head above the turbulent waters of abject personal misery had become a fulltime occupation, and now he was most definitely sinking.

With a measure of equal reluctance and duty, he accepted her suggestion.

"I shall have to know her name if she is to live here," he instructed.

"Bess, Sir."

"Go inside, girl. Now."

Annoying Robert with her interruption, the mother grabbed the girl just as she started to walk. Turning her daughter back round to face her, she said soothingly:

"Here, take this."

In her child's hand, she dropped a small metal brooch and tearfully whispered:

"Remember me, child."

Keen to avoid any further embarrassment, Mr Harvey ushered the girl in, muttering:

"Goodbye, vicar—madam." as the door slowly closed.

Peering behind the parlour curtain, Robert saw the vicar leading the poor heartbroken wretch away, supporting her at the elbow as she weakly staggered along. Soon all that was left were shallow footprints in the gravel path leading to Walton Hall; and of course, the girl.

3

THE CUCKOO'S EGG ARRIVES

"The matter is settled" announced Mr Harvey over a tense evening meal. "The girl will move in. I will hear no more of your protestations."

This latest saga in the Harvey household had been an almighty shock to everyone: the spouse, the siblings, the servants, and the straying husband too. No one was exempt from the profound frayed nerves and tempers. It had been a very tense day.

Mr and Mrs Harvey retreated to the parlour as they directed the children to go to their rooms. They ordered the servants to clear the dining room table after the evening meal, and then have a second attempt at cleaning up Bess. Although she smelled better after the first rushed attempt, Robert's inspection of her before dinner highlighted that her nails still had dark crescents of dirt around them and her hair was tangled and unkempt. The child still had the air of a slum-dwelling urchin about her, even though she had come from the hillside.

Angrily, Robert turned to his spouse, taking big gulps of whiskey from the glass in his hand. *My wife has been a shrew to live with for years, and now things are yet more rancorous.*

He knew she was going to point out where their wealth came from yet again, always trying to undermine him, questioning his ability to provide for his family like a proper, respectable man. It was one of the things that had first driven a wedge between them, years ago.

> "So, two indiscretions have surfaced in rapid succession. What kind of a man are you?" scolded Mrs Harvey

> "I shall tell you what kind of a man I am, Madam. In the eyes of the law, I am the head of this household, and you will respect me. You are my wife who has, of late, forgotten where her place is in Walton Hall. Your place is to love, honour and obey, may I remind you. Yet, all I get is coldness, criticism, and never support."

Hannah's eyes blazed with rage as her husband continued to share his side of the story.

> "Your choice, night after night, to spurn me is what prompted my straying from the marital bed. Your behaviour is what has caused these—"

"—betrayals—?" she interrupted with anger.

"—liaisons! Endless long, cold days and nights with you have driven me into these warm women's arms. What is a man to do, if a wife rejects his advances? If you had welcomed me more often, I would not have needed to look outside of wedlock for my manly comforts."

Hannah's nostrils flared as she reached for a heavy statue on the mantelpiece, preparing to throw it at him, to hurt him as he had her.

Quick as a fox, Mr Harvey grabbed her hand and squeezed the wrist so tightly the pain forced her to relinquish her grip before she could even lift it. He raised a hand to slap her, to prove her subordinacy but thought better of it.

"Fear not! I understand, husband. I will retain an air of quiet composure as your illegitimate spawn weasels her way into our home. Do you know, her selfish mother is like a cuckoo that lays its egg in the nest and poisons the place for all other souls within it."

I so want to strike this woman, but it will only make the acrimony worse. The arguments that have filled the house will not abate any quicker if I use my fists. Hannah may be many things, but she is not stupid. Surely, she knows I can overpower and overrule her at will. Why does she persist in fighting back? Why not show some loyalty? And by God, I would far prefer a supportive wife at the moment, rather than the sniping, griping harpy I am reluctantly wedded to. I need more whiskey.

Hannah's mind was full of dismay and what-ifs as she watched him pour almost a full tumbler of the golden-yellow liquor.

How has life come to this? Damn you, Father, for throwing me to Robert Harvey like a Roman emperor tossed a Christian to a lion for entertainment. Did he not care? Surely, he could have secured a better alliance given our wealth?

She decided to claw back a modicum of control by announcing a carefully considered concession.

"I shall give you the fake veneer of respectability in public, Robert. She can stay under certain conditions. She will not be brought up with our children. She will receive a basic level of care from the servant girls. They can teach her the ways of servitude. You must recognise we lack the funds to treat her the same way as our—legitimate—children. She can earn her keep helping with the household chores. She may be your child, Robert, but she most certainly is not mine."

The man of the house stayed silent, topping his pipe with fresh tobacco to keep his angry hands busy.

"We will tell people that she is a distant relative—cruelly orphaned—and that we have taken her in as decent people. She will attend church in good clothes, hand-me-downs from Harriet or Nell, perhaps? But for the rest of the time, she will be confined to the house, hard at work. Those are my terms. If you do not agree to this, I will perhaps have to ask my father to consider if he wishes to subsidise our business any longer. As you know, he is at the end of his patience with you and your feckless decisions. Hearing you take in your love-child will be the last straw."

Robert Harvey continued to drink heavily. It was the only solace he had available.

Mrs Harvey knew her husband could not argue with her logic. Loathing the reappearance of his characteristic intimidating stare, she left the room to seek some respite from it. She closed the door loudly behind her to show her contempt and then walked directly to the servants' quarters.

She found them, brushing the wretched child's hair, and affixing a bonnet tightly around it, desperately trying to tame it into some sort of style. Out of the wet rags that she arrived in, they had dressed her in an ill-fitting servants' uniform, which was going to need a lot of taking in to make it fit her small frame.

Mrs Harvey looked on with contempt. *She will learn her place, and it is not on her father's knee. Out of sight, out of mind, is going to be the best policy.*

"Ladies, I am sure I do not need to remind you there will be no talk of the truth about this girl outside this house. If your tongues wag, even utter one word, I will find out, and you will be sacked. Do you hear me?"

"Yes, Ma'am," they said in unison.

Disobeying the vengeful lady of the house was always the root to more hardship.

"Not only will you be immediately dismissed for any indiscretion, but I will make sure that people in the area know that you are dishonest, disrespectful and unreliable. I shall tell them you stole valuables from this household and that is why you have been let go. If some busybody wants to poke their nose into our business, the girl is an orphan from a distant branch of the family we have taken in to raise as our own. Is that clear?"

"Yes, Ma'am."

"But— she will not be one of our own. She will be one of you. You shall train her to be a productive member of staff. I shall be expecting you to act, in loco parentis, as her guardians. My husband and I will have nothing to do with her. Is that clear?"

The servants nodded.

Mrs Harvey swooped towards the front door, putting on her coat as she left, without announcing her departure.

She was off to see the vicar to ask for his discretion in this 'delicate matter'.

On her return, she found the children's door open. They were listening out for her.

Up to that point, the Harveys had three children: a son, Richard, the eldest, aged thirteen, then a daughter, Harriet, aged twelve, and the youngest at just ten, Nell.

"Children, come to the parlour—Now!"

She sat them down in the dimly lit room, red flock wallpaper and velvet curtains eating what little light came from outside. She lit a couple of oil lamps to banish the gloom.

Before the children could utter a single word, Hannah forbade them to associate with Bess. She repeated the rules about her enforced separation and that she would live with the servants.

"Your father may have decided to show benevolence, but I shall not. Woe betide you if I find out you are associating with that loathsome child."

The door creaked open, and Robert Harvey stood at the doorway. He had heard her poisonous proclamation in full.

"Leave! Now!" he barked, triggering terror in the innocent children's faces. Sensing his mistake, he quickly added in a calmer voice, "Go on. Go to your rooms. I wish to talk to your mother in private."

It was time for Mr Harvey to assert his authority. Clasping his wife by the elbow, he frogmarched her to the bedroom and closed the door, thereby signalling they were not to be interrupted. *It is time to put an end to my wife's dissent and disobedience.*

"I appreciate that this is an unpleasant business, Hannah, but I must do right by the child. To support my new responsibilities, I plan to visit my brother for the week to discuss a resolution to the colliery's troubles. He has had greater success in the industry than I. Together, I am sure we can solve 'my' predicament with the pit's profitability. I trust you now recognise 'our' predicament with the child is resolved?"

Without waiting for a reply, he extinguished the oil lamps in the bedroom and got into bed and lay flat on his back. Within minutes there was a loud rasping noise, like a heavy corpse giving out its last. A foetid smell of smoke and drink-laden breath filled the darkness.

Hannah lay, precariously balanced on the very edge of her side of the bed, silent tears soaking into her pillow.

No one in the house believed sleeping on their problems that night would make the next day any easier to bear.

In the morning, Robert Harvey travelled to see his brother, hoping that things would calm down in his week-long absence.

4

THE BROKEN VASE

The sudden demand to be the guardian of her errant husband's illegitimate child weighed heavily on Hannah. There was nothing for it but to go for a morning walk to clear her head and escape the oppressive mood in the household.

She put on her coat and made her way into the large garden behind the hall. Pacing back and forth along the long paths, she pondered her situation. Sometimes the answer to some of life's most challenging problems had a habit of wafting into her mind, drawn in by the fresh air and space.

As she was dusting the dining room window sill, Bess had seen her stepmother leave the hall. *She's a good two hundred yards away. That gives me a few minutes to wander through the rooms to learn more about this new family—of mine.*

Bess had been feeling lost, wondering if her mother might come back and collect her once her health improved and she had perhaps found a husband. *Maybe the vicar had helped her somehow so she could avoid the dreaded workhouse.* It was unlikely, but the white lie she told herself was much more palatable than the truth.

In the dining room was a portrait of a smartly dressed man, Mr Harvey's father by the looks of it. In his advancing years, he looked very grand. Powerful. He wore a long tailored, black coat and matching hat. The rich shiny paint of his white shirt almost glowed. The man looked strong and healthy. In the far distance of the painting, were some rolling hills and another impressive Georgian stately home with three floors. *Clearly, the Harvey's have been extremely wealthy in the past. Walton Hall is impressive, but that house is almost palatial.*

As she walked upstairs, she could hear the other children singing around the piano, with Harriet suggesting ditties she could play for them. Along the staircase wall were more impressive family portraits.

At the top of the landing was her father's study.

She looked and listened in earnest to check the room was empty. Hoping she would be undetected, with a faint rasp of its straining hinges, she pushed the heavy door open. Inside were rows and rows of books on shelves. Her father was clearly a learned man. There were decorative ornaments dotted around the room, most of them expensive-looking Bateman silverware, plus white-and-blue Delftware ceramics although, Bess the ragged urchin that she was, was unaware of their impressive provenance. Even though their precise origin eluded her, they did confirm the family's prosperity. She was now living in a household with more wealth than she could have ever dreamt of in her lifetime. The contrast with the shepherd's hut she had been raised in was dizzying.

To give her a cover story for sneaking upstairs, she carefully took out a dusty cut-crystal vase from an ornate display cabinet and prepared to clean within the grooves. As the cloth glided over the delicate surface, Bess's mind drifted to her dramatic change in circumstances, and that perhaps, one day, she would have a share of the Harvey's riches. She was wholly absorbed by the cacophony of conflicting ideas in her head.

And then bang. The study door swung fully open and smashed loudly against the doorstop, there to protect the smooth plaster from the ravages of the metal door handle. Shocked by the sudden noise, Bess's little hands trembled, fumbled, then dropped the vase. In horror, she looked at the shattered pieces on the floor. She prayed it was a breeze that had caught the door. Turning her head to the entrance, she saw a thunderous Mrs Harvey glaring at her. Bess stuttered a genuine apology, but it was no use. Hannah was livid, brimming with an uncontrollable rage.

Striding over she howled:

"Now look what you've done, you stupid child. I did not want you in this house before, and now I want you here even less."

The back of her hand rose up towards the ceiling, like a bird of prey eyeing its target, then it swooped down, striking the child across the cheek. The sting was so painful little Bess almost collapsed.

"That vase belonged to my grandmother. It came from Venice—not that someone of your upbringing would know where that is. Your clumsiness will not go unpunished. Further, if you cannot be a good servant, then there is no place for you in this house, and I will do my utmost to see that you are removed."

In a furious temper, she grabbed Bess and slapped the girl's thighs with each word as she screeched:

"Stop—Your—Snivelling—"

Once Mrs Harvey let go, Bess tried to pick up the shards of glass to make amends, but it was no use. She cut her thumb as she scrabbled about on the floor desperately trying to show remorse. Drops of blood began to stain the light-coloured flooring, angering Hannah further still.

"You are determined to ruin everything! I will not tolerate it. Do you hear me! I will speak to my husband on his return and explain that you are not to be trusted. I want you out of my sight."

She grabbed Bess roughly by the hair, almost pulling her over. Then she seized the sobbing child's left arm savagely, hauling it upwards, as she propelled her back downstairs towards the servants' area. It felt like the force would dislocate her shoulder.

Seeing Meg in the corridor, she ordered her into action.

"Please attend to the mess in the study caused by this careless child."

Before Meg even had the chance to turn to face her mistress, her ears rang out as Hannah screamed, "Immediately!" and at that, she scuttled off.

Alone with Bess, Hannah continued.

"We are having a family picnic at the weekend. I want you to go and prepare our boathouse by the lake. The table and chairs have not been used over the winter months. I suspect even a foozler like you couldn't smash our wooden possessions as you dust them, Go. Now. I do not want to see you in Walton Hall until nightfall."

She took the child and dragged her to the back door, leading onto the garden.

Sobbing and stumbling, Bess made her way down the gravel path towards the twee chalet-style building at the end. She was glad the lady of the house hadn't followed her, for fear of another beating. Her cheek and legs were still hot and stinging from the previous thrashing.

Bess was surprised to find the door unlocked and slightly ajar. She made her way tentatively inside. As her eyes adjusted to the darkness, she could see three boats being stored, two on the wall, one laying on the floor, close to the entrance, to the left of the folded picnic tables and chairs. The dust was so thick, Bess could have written her name in it, had she known how to write.

There was a pile of soft, folded rags at the far corner of the boathouse that would make for dusters.

Suddenly, she heard footsteps on the gravel path. It was her stepmother. It had to be. The children had been told to ignore her. Meg and Sarah were busy preparing food. But rather than come in and threaten her again, Mrs Harvey stood at the doorway, silent for a few moments, watching Bess. *She must be observing me? I'd better show I can be trusted to follow orders to the letter since my first blunder was so rapidly discovered.*

In the privacy of the boathouse, Mrs Harvey unleashed her wrath once more. She took one of the small wooden oars from the rack on the wall. Bess, fearing another brutal beating, tried to run away.

Hannah swung the oar like a warden would use the birch on a prisoner. Doing her utmost to dodge the blow, the young girl lost her footing and tripped over the edge of the small rowing boat on the floor.

She tumbled and banged her head hard on the corner of the solid wooden stern. Dazed and blinking hard, she tried to clear her vision.

Alas, there was no point. The door slammed behind her, and she was alone in the darkness. She heard a piece of wood slide across some metal latches outside, wedging the door solidly in place, and then the twist of a heavy key in the lock made sure there would be no escape.

"You shall stay in there until you learn your place, my girl."

The footsteps went away. A severely injured Bess drifted in and out of consciousness. As night fell, the cold air finally brought her fully around. She was famished and petrified.

She pulled a rough, dusty tarpaulin around herself and made a small pillow with her apron. Her attempts at sleep were fitful, being woken repeatedly by panic, hunger and sadness.

As dawn broke, she felt steady enough to get back on her feet.

Forgetting about the wooden latch, she tried to push the key out of the lock with a small stick she'd found, hoping it would fall close to the doorway, where she could drag it inside with her nimble little fingers. The key tumbled out but landed just out of reach.

She shook the door and shouted for help, too distressed to fear the consequences anymore. *Whatever happened, things can't get any worse. Perhaps their gardener might hear me. The Harveys seem wealthy enough to have one perhaps? None of the family members will be out until breakfast is finished, at the earliest.*

The shouting made her voice hoarse, and her hands gained a fair few splinters as she did her best to beat on the door for help.

Sad, trapped and alone, Bess wished with all her heart she could be reunited with her mother, a soul who loved the bones of her unconditionally.

5

THE POACHER IN THE BOATHOUSE

From sunrise, Harry Sutherland, the young eighteen-year-old gamekeeper at Lord Hamilton's country pile had been patrolling the edge of the estate. In places, it bordered the grounds of Walton Hall. There had been a lot of trouble of late with poaching. A daily inspection had been ordered to check for any signs of forced entry to the lord's land.

Being well-versed in the art of hunting, Harry had excellent hearing. He turned his head to one side, towards the unfamiliar sound, to listen more clearly. *There it was again. A loud rattle is coming from the Harvey's boathouse. Perhaps an injured robber has sheltered in there from the cold night air and got stuck?*

Lord Hamilton had requested a plethora of mantraps to be installed, particularly around the perimeter of his estate to protect his livestock and game. *If the rapscallions have come as a pair, a partner in crime could release his accomplice, although they wouldn't get far with that badly mangled leg.* As he got nearer, he could also hear weeping. *Hmm. Poachers never give out high-pitched sobs, injured or not.*

He tip-toed over to the boathouse and saw the key on the floor. He tried to peer through one of the cracks between the planks of wood making up the walls, but it was too dark to see inside. *What the devil's gone on here?*

He took the key, put it in the lock, then slid the wooden plank from its metal latches.

"Who's there? Speak up?" he asked before opening the door.

"Me, Mister. Please 'elp me! Please!"

On hearing the voice, Harry Sutherland jumped into action and threw the door open.

Near the entrance, he saw a small, petrified, servant girl blinking at the early-morning light streaming in. She looked more like a cornered animal than a human being. Trapped in the darkness, she hadn't realised that blood had steadily seeped everywhere from her head wound. She looked in quite a state.

The soft skin on her forehead, cheek and jowls felt stiff and crackly as she smiled at the stranger. Flakes of it came away as she rubbed it, thinking it was dried-on dirt from the floor.

He unfolded one of the picnic chairs and sat down, then lifted her onto his knee. She wrapped her arms around his neck and buried her face in the soft curve of his skin. He could tell from her behaviour she was most grateful to be found.

With a kindly voice, he asked:

"Are you hungry, Miss? I bet you are—"

Feeling her head nod against his neck, he offered her a few bites of half a cheese sandwich he'd carried in his knapsack to fuel his lengthy patrol of the Hamilton estate.

As Bess chomped down on it, ravenous, it soon vanished. Harry thought it best to offer the other half too under the circumstances.

"Thanks, Mister. You are too kind."

Sutherland thought it difficult not to be, given that whoever was supposed to be looking after the girl at Walton Hall, was acting with such wilful neglect. She still seemed a lively, pretty young soul, despite the poor treatment. She had a certain charm about her and didn't deserve to be locked away like a farmyard beast.

"What are you doin' in here, Miss?" the young gamekeeper asked.

Reluctant to confide in a stranger, risking bringing more shame on her new guardians should word travel, she thought it best to lie.

"I'm a servant from the 'ouse. I was sent on an errand to make it nice in 'ere for the weekend. The door blew shut, and I was stuck. I 'ad 'oped they would come for me, but maybe they forgot?"

Knowing that even the strongest of winds couldn't blow a plank through the door latches by itself, Harry didn't fall for her tale. No nearer ascertaining the truth, one thing was clear, someone at Walton Hall had taken a strong dislike to this young ragamuffin.

Changing the subject, he asked:

"So—what's your name? I'm Harry. Harry Sutherland."

"Elizabeth, but folks call me Bess." she replied with a cheeky smile, preferring not to add the 'arvey' just yet.

"Right then, Bess, you seem a bit steadier on your feet now. Let's get you back to Walton, shall we? Best get you cleaned up a bit first though? You'll scare 'em half to death with all that blood on yer. We'll go via the back door, avoid causin' a scene. Tongues wag in

Woodborough, Miss. You never know whose beady eyes are upon you."

As they walked back to the hall, they stopped at a small stone birdbath. Harry dipped his checked handkerchief into the water then gently dabbed at Bess's face. By her hairline was a deepish cut about an inch long. The patting caused the freshly formed scab to weaken, and she started to bleed again. Anxious he'd made things worse, Harry kept quiet and asked Bess to press the handkerchief against her head as they walked, hoping the scab would close up quickly again. He fretted that if anyone saw them, he might be accused of injuring the girl with a mind to act inappropriately with her.

With reluctance, a miserable Bess trundled a pace or two behind him, back towards the hall.

'ow can I explain my absence and unexpected arrival to Meg; she's sure to be up by now, preparing the fires for the day. I'll be in even more trouble for wandering off. I'm supposed to be 'elping 'er with all the chores!

"Please don't tell anyone about wot's 'appened. I'm already in so much bother. Broke an expensive vase yesterday. The mistress was livid. If she kicks me out, I 'ave nothing. I need this employment at the 'all else I'll end up in the Union."

So, it seems like it's Mrs Harvey that's got it in for her. A grown woman roughing up a mere child like that. Tsch.

"Right you are, Miss. Workhouse is no place for you—
. No place for anybody—" he trailed off.

Near the end of the path by the back door, he whispered:

"Off you trot then," keen to see his unexpected ward
returned safely to the house.

From behind the hedge, he watched her go through the
door and left towards the scullery. Through the window,
he saw another servant girl swoop to her aid, kneeling
down and talking to her, casting a worried eye over her
wound. Satisfied he had done what he could, he swiftly
returned to Lord Hamilton's woodland that he was supposed to be guarding before his absence was noted too.

6

THE SECRET

Whilst it was quick for the servants to rinse and dry the girl's clothes, the nasty wound on her head was going to need attention.

"'ow are we going to tell Mrs 'arvey, Meg? It's clear she's taken a deep disliking to the child," asked Sarah. "What if this 'ere injury is serious, and she takes a turn for the worse? The master will surely get rid of us. How did we not know she was missing all night? From a distance, I honestly thought that lump in her bed was her, not ruckled up fabric around a pillow. What are we to do?"

As the most senior of the household staff, Meg plucked up the courage to broach the subject when she brought the lady of the house her early breakfast.

"I think we need to call the doctor, Ma'am."

Mrs Harvey raised an eyebrow at her boldness.

"Yes, Ma'am. The young urchin has 'urt herself. Taken a blow to the forehead somehow. She must 'ave been wandering in the dark at night, got 'erself lost and taken a tumble. The wound keeps bleeding. We can't seem to stop it for long."

"That mongrel of a girl is a drain on this household. Breaking priceless possessions yesterday. Needing to see the doctor today. No. We will manage the situation ourselves, Meg. Get Sarah to bandage it. Keep some pressure on until it stops."

"Yes, Ma'am."

"And get her a bonnet to cover the dressing. I will not have Mr Harvey worried by this."

"As you wish," Meg confirmed.

"Now get out of my sight, before my breakfast is stone cold."

Meg retreated back to the servants' quarters. It had been a tense, loveless atmosphere at Walton Hall for quite a while, but it had grown icier since news of Mr Harvey's infidelities had surfaced.

Hannah roundly attacked the shell of her boiled egg with the back of her spoon. The cracks formed a dented recess in the top that was quickly scooped away, exposing the runny yellow yolk within. Despite her staunch countenance, inside she was crumbling. *How could Robert be so beastly? So ungrateful? It is my father's wealth that has supported this family, saved us from bankruptcy, propped up the colliery. I gave him my body freely and produced three healthy children.* She bit her lip til it hurt, trying to fight back the tears brought about more by anger than frustration.

Back in the servants' quarters, after Bess's wound was dressed for the third time, then camouflaged with a white bonnet sporting a sizeable, droopy frill, the servants busied themselves choosing chores that would keep them out of the way of Mrs Harvey.

They were drawn out of their hiding place later that morning when, on the driveway, Mr Harvey's black carriage pulled up after his week-long visit to his brother. They discreetly peered out of a window to assess the master's mood. He got out and made his way to the house. It was difficult to see his face clearly from their vantage point.

He heaved open the hefty front door with one arm, his other holding a plump briefcase to his side. He stood in the hallway, listening out for who might be around. There was silence. Wondering where everyone was, he decided to tilt his head around every door until he found his family. He was tired of the bellowing that had filled the house of late. The children were alone, reading.

He greeted them, then made his way to the study, keen to set down the heavy bag.

Looking through the window towards the garden, he saw Hannah pacing along the path, keeping warm in her fur hat and shawl. *She always walks when she has something on her mind. That thing must be Bess. I bet she's hiding something that's gone on in my absence.*

The only place left to look for Bess was with the other servants. She clearly wasn't working on chores in the house. He made his way to their quarters.

"Where is my daughter?" he demanded, trying to be civil, but failing.

"Why she's resting, Sir."

"Resting? Why she not helping you? She must earn her keep. I may have shown compassion and taken her in, but I am not running a charity. She needs to work."

After an awkward pause, Meg volunteered:

"She's injured—Sir."

"Injured? How? Did I not ask you to take care of her? Was she scalded in the kitchen? Hands trapped in a mangle?"

"No, Sir."

"Take me to her now. I want to assess her condition myself."

"Yes, Mr 'arvey."

An icy procession paced to the servants' shared bedroom. As the door opened, the two women excused themselves:

"We'll leave you be, Sir."

Robert gazed around the drab bluey-grey walls, with only a few personal effects on display: a vase of wildflowers and a handful of embroidery miniatures to soften the bleakness.

At the far wall, was Bess, curled up in bed, trying to disappear under the covers.

"There you are! Meg tells me you are injured!"

"It was my fault, Father, I promise. I did something silly."

She told her father about the errand at the end of the garden, and confessed to tripping, but did not mention Mrs Harvey locking her into the boathouse overnight, nor needing to be rescued by the kind-hearted gamekeeper from the neighbouring estate.

She was petrified Mr Harvey may renege on his promise to her mother. *The less said about the tensions between my stepmother and me, the better.*

Seeing the bandage on her head, Robert wanted to look at it, but she squirmed away, ashamed that she had not taken better care of herself. Sensing her angst, he kissed his fingertips instead and rested them on the bandaged bump below the frilly, white bonnet.

The tenderness gave Bess hope that perhaps, something could be salvaged from this awful mess. Mrs Harvey seemed to tend to her own children well. *Perhaps one day she will accept me?* Then with a sigh, more thoughts bubbled up to the surface. *Oh, don't be so stupid, Bess. Keep quiet. Keep your head down. Mother might come back for you soon. And if she can't, Meg and Sarah will take care of you, teach you how to be a good servant. Then as soon as you are old enough, you could work somewhere else, away from the malicious Mrs Harvey.*

"I do find it strange my wife would talk of a weekend picnic in these colder months of the year. I shall speak to her about the matter."

Bess's heart sank.

Robert Harvey knew his wife's cruelty was underpinning this fiasco. She was always self-centred. Like the cold, calculating men in her family, selfishness was how they had prospered in the world of business.

He turned to leave, giving Bess a broad smile, before disappearing out towards the garden to find his wife. Hearing the crunch of footsteps on the greyish-white gravel, Hannah turned around.

"You have some explaining to do, Madam." hissed Robert. "My daughter has been badly injured while she has been in your care. And I would like for you to explain why? It seems she was running a curious unnecessary errand for you at the boathouse. The servants have told me that they have done their best to attend to her, and I believe them. If anyone has a reason for harm to come to that child, it is you."

Inside, a curious Meg and Sarah spied the angry exchange taking place as the furious couple returned to the house. They walked upstairs in silence, with Mrs Harvey just managing to lock herself in their bedroom before Robert could stop her.

Tired of arguing, and feeling the pressure of the financial worries caused by the troubled colliery, he decided to return to the pit that afternoon to reflect on his brother's advice.

He asked for Meg to make some sandwiches saying he would not have time to dine with the family that evening since he would be finishing late. That was partly true. He neglected to mention his wife's lack of understanding was driving him to despair, and he couldn't bear being in the same house as her.

Meg nodded in agreement, keen not to disappoint the master in his aggravated state, and immediately set about her task.

"I'll bring them up to you, Sir, as soon as they're ready."

He collected the papers he needed together. About thirty minutes later, he heard his bedroom door quietly click as the lock was released.

Robert seized the moment and waltzed in to see his wife.

"Enjoy dining alone tonight, Hannah. Your selfishness has taken my appetite. I suggest you reflect on your atrocious behaviour in my absence. You're worse than a prison matron. I shall not forget the harm you caused Bess. She may be thought of as an orphan outside of this household, and she is not of your blood, but I will not have her mistreated. Do you understand?" he snapped.

He raised his hand and slapped his wife roughly across the face so hard that she fell on the bed as he reprimanded her.

"You disgust me. I suggest you choose to support rather than undermine me in future. There is no wonder I seek comfort with other ladies when I am stuck with a cold, heartless, woman like you."

An angry Hannah stared at him in shock, still clutching her throbbing cheek.

A few minutes later, there was a slam of the front door, and his carriage pulled away.

It would be almost midnight when Robert Harvey staggered back into the hallway, roaring drunk, having quaffed most of another bottle of whiskey throughout the journey home, desperate to drown the dark thoughts and bleak circumstances that dragged him down.

7

TWO HEADS ARE
BETTER THAN ONE

With a thick head the following morning, Mr Harvey wondered if his growing mountain of woes would ever abate. Problems seemed to seek him out like flies around the eyes of a horse.

He took his breakfast in the dining room, in silence, with his wife and the children. The doorbell rang to announce the arrival of his elder brother, fifteen years his senior. David was aware of the problems of the pit, but blissfully unaware of the strife at home. He quickly sensed the atmosphere on his arrival.

"Would you like some breakfast, Mr Harvey?" queried Sarah, showing him to the dining room.

"That would be wonderful. I had a very early start to get here today."

He turned to Robert, saying:

"You did tell me that the matter was urgent—"

"Indeed, it is," he replied.

Hannah finished her last mouthfuls of breakfast and excused herself. David took her place at the table.

The two men started to discuss business. One by one, the children finished their food. At last, David and Robert were alone, sharing some tea, and what was on their minds.

Robert was determined to keep the conversation focused on the colliery.

"So, to recap from our discussions last week, I have invested heavily in some modern equipment to improve our productivity above ground, getting coal carts to the railway depot more quickly, but that has been at the expense of financial security. Our cash reserves are depleted, and so too is our colliery. Our older seams are becoming less profitable. The men are becoming quite surly about it since their income is dropping with such slim pickings of coal being brought to the surface for their efforts. We need the hewers to explore new, deeper, areas if the mine is to return to profit, but they are having their ears turned by the petulant labour movement, and would rather work elsewhere than take the risk of going the extra mile for me. They are becoming more militant about working conditions. They're right. This mine is an accident waiting to happen."

"This has always been a concern, Robert. You clearly inherited the more difficult colliery of the two from Father. I was lucky. I am sure we can fix it. Let's continue where we left off last week. Two heads are better than one—" he trailed off.

Robert stirred his tea, looking drained.

"I can tell there's something else, weighing on your mind—what is it?" asked his brother, delicately.

"It's nothing. Let us fix the colliery. That is my priority."

David made some notes on paper as Robert stared into space, his head pounding from the excesses with the drink the day before.

Distracted, they didn't hear the door creaking open an inch at a time. Still unaware of the proper protocol, Bess had come in to collect the breakfast plates, thinking the silence had meant the room was vacant.

Once inside, she saw the two men's heads rise and turn to see who was there.

David was shocked at the likeness of the young girl in front of him. Immediately, he realised what was causing his brother's recent brooding disposition and the worsening hostility from his wife.

"I'm sorry, Sir," said Bess excusing herself, scurrying away down the corridor.

"Come, let's go to the study and discuss how to fix your troubles."

Bess heard the two sets of footsteps go along the hallway, then up the stairs. She quickly returned to collect the breakfast plates for fear of another beating if Mrs Harvey found them first. Carefully, she stacked her tray so that she didn't cause any more breakages.

Robert Harvey gently closed the study door behind him. The two brothers spoke in hushed tones so that they would not be overheard.

"So— explain this new 'servant' to me, Robert. You have two servants for this household already. That is plenty, given your financial state. Why take on another?"

David was playing devil's advocate. He wanted to see if his brother told the truth, for the likeness was undeniable.

"I expect you've worked it out, David. Yes, you're correct. She is my child. Her mother lived up near the colliery—in the shepherd's cottage? I sometimes encountered her sat on the hillside, staring out at the sunset, alone. I found Mary's beauty quite alluring. We often—"

He stopped to clear his throat.

"—The girl's mother became gravely ill recently, and with the death of her own father, she had no option but the workhouse. She travelled to Woodborough and asked the vicar where Walton Hall was—turned up on the doorstep and foisted the child on me. I believe the parish was not able to give outside support for her and the child since they were now homeless and with no other relatives. Committal was, therefore, the only option.

David listened without giving any clues about his opinion on the latest developments.

"I don't need to tell you that things have been difficult here, David. My wife sees fit to remind me that I am a failure on a daily basis—that I am squandering her money—disrespecting her family—with my poor business decisions and the like. But as you know, Britain is the biggest supplier of coal in the world. There is more than enough demand. And, although the colliery has been difficult to manage, the coal industry is moving apace, and lucrative. The profits will come soon. I know it."

"I agree." said his brother finally showing some sympathy.

"And I also know that a cold wife leads to a cold bed. Men have hot-blooded needs that cannot be suppressed. What did she think would happen if she spurned your physical advances? You would become a monk?"

Robert nodded with relief that David had chosen to side with him. That said, when it came to adultery, brothers always did.

"I don't blame you, Robert. You are of human flesh, a real man. And you are proving that manhood by making good, supporting your child. No one would want their own flesh and blood in the workhouse if it were within their power to prevent it. And you have space to take her on here in the servants' quarters. Even if she can't become a proper daughter like your other two, life in your servitude until she reaches adulthood will at least mean she can escape the Union and you can offer extra help when you can."

Keen to bring the conversation to an end, David added:

"Now, I think that is enough talk about your household troubles. Apart from one last matter."

Robert was grateful for his brother's support. Quite a contrast from the tongue lashings his wife kept doling out.

He was still unsure of his children's feelings about the urchin although he suspected, because of their youth, they might be more tolerant and common-sense would prevail; and so far, they seemed to have kept his secret from the chinwaggers of Woodborough.

Assuming Hannah might be walking in the garden to escape the atmosphere, as usual, they began to speak a little louder. Today, however, deliberately returning early, she crept outside the study door and had her head almost pressed against it, her curiosity getting the better of her. She heard David speaking.

"Take this. It's all the money I have with me. It will help you buy some extra food and clothes the child, for if she is your flesh and blood, she's also mine."

Robert was silenced by his brother's unanticipated show of generosity.

He just managed to tuck the thick roll of notes in his slim waistcoat pocket, as he opened the door for his brother, in readiness to escort him back to the entrance.

Hearing David so readily accept the child had made Hannah seethe, freezing her to the spot with anger. Ambushed by the unexpected opening of the door, she was found eavesdropping.

Slipping instinctively into defence mode, Robert spoke first.

"So, it seems my brother has accepted the child, wife. For heaven's sake, can you not too?

She turned to go to the bedroom, and her husband followed her.

A minute later, he came out to see David to apologise for a slight delay as he dealt with 'the situation'.

Before he said anything, the elder brother stepped in.

"Let me go ahead to the colliery, Robert. I can speak to the pitmaster. Join me when you can. Let's say before noon?"

He could sense the hostility deepening between his brother and sister-in-law since faint sobs were emanating from behind the bedroom door. Hannah was making a bad job of crying quietly into her pillow today, despite a lot of practice of late.

After finishing another heated debate, Robert left for the mine. The children and Hannah kept themselves busy around the piano, with his wife barking the lyrics and dishing out harsh feedback on their delivery, reprimanding them for singing just one note out of tune.

It was seven o'clock in the evening when Robert returned. The meal was eaten in complete silence. No one wanted to say anything for fear of an argument.

The children went to bed, and the strained husband and wife retired to the parlour.

Mrs Harvey jabbed at the fabric of her embroidery. Her husband poured a series of large whiskeys and puffed at a huge cigar in silence. Both were deep in thought, plotting their next move.

Hannah retired first, not wanting to get changed into her nightdress in front of her loathsome, straying husband. He followed on fifteen minutes later, then spent considerable time preparing his clothes for the next day. His wife pretended to sleep, pulling the covers so high up, they almost covered her entire face.

He got changed into a loose nightshirt and made his way to the bed, extinguishing all but one of the oil lamps. As he landed heavily on the mattress and slung his legs under the sheets, Hannah buried her head fully under the covers. Reaching across, he snatched the material away and grabbed her by the shoulder, forcing her onto her back. She turned her head away, clearly not consenting to his advances.

Wanting to pin her to the bed, he put his other hand on her forehead and held her firmly. He pressed his mouth roughly onto hers. *She will love, honour and obey me.*

Fighting against her drunken husband, she finally managed to free her mouth.

"You are a monster."

He ignored her protestations, gripping even more tightly as he made the most of his opportunity to claim his conjugal rights. Afterwards, he extinguished the last oil lamp, returned to bed and rolled over, also preferring the far edge, and quickly fell asleep.

She lay staring at the ceiling alone, with tears trickling down from the corners of her eyes and down over the tops of her ears, grateful for the darkness that hid the brute next to her.

8

THE EXILE OF BESS

Robert Harvey had spent the early hours, lying awake, feeling angry. The hand of cards he had been dealt had not stacked in his favour. Keen to get away from Hannah, he got out of bed and paced around his study where he knew he would be alone.

That morning he was on a mission.

He stopped at various points around the room, picking up antique ornaments, inspecting them, looking for distinguishing marks and defects. He squinted at each one through one eye, pretending to be an expert trying to establish its value.

His task was to find some things that could be sold to fund Bess's education, at least in the short term. He felt home life for her was horrid. He didn't want Bess to be raised in such a hateful environment, even if she was illegitimate. *Surely, she will be better at boarding school,*

they will do an excellent job of turning her into a lady, and
nobody needs to know her humble background.

Sitting down at his desk, deep in thought, he pushed the fingers of both hands through his thick hair as he studied the family's finances. He hoped with the sale of a handful of precious heirlooms he could afford the eighteen guineas a year school fees.

He collected together a selection of carefully packed possessions, all antique silverware, hid them in his briefcase, and took his haul by train to the nearby town of Westbridge, conveniently close by, but still far enough away for him not to be recognised. He wanted to keep this matter private. Some of the valuables were his wife's property, not his, things her father had given them as wedding presents to put on display in their new matrimonial home. He found it amusing that Hannah was indirectly paying for Bess's advancement in life.

Robert smiled to himself when Walter Brown, the antique dealer, carefully counted out the proceeds of their transaction. His visit had been worth his while. He stuffed a copious amount of cash into his now empty briefcase, closed it securely then clutched the handle tightly. Briskly, he made his way back to the station, his mind rehearsing the two crucial conversations he needed to have on his return.

Back at Walton Hall, he darted upstairs to the study then closed the door, keen to hide the money from prying eyes. With that done, it was time to navigate the first of the two discussions.

He summoned Hannah to the study doing his best to be polite. She stepped into the room and quietly closed the door behind her, anticipating another argument over the child.

Robert, sat behind his desk, invited her to sit in the chair opposite. His sudden warmth was very disconcerting after the events in the marital bed the night before.

"I've come up with a compromise, Hannah. I've decided to send Bess away to boarding school. I cannot concentrate with this atmosphere in the house. It is draining. I agree, it is clear from her demeanour that Bess has had a less fortunate upbringing to our offspring and I believe sending her to boarding school will make it easier for me—us—to turn her into a young lady and find her a suitable husband when the time comes."

Unable to look Robert in the eye, Hannah had been gazing around the room, sensing something different, but not quite knowing what.

"Seeing the departure of that ungainly child would be a delight, Robert. But given the problems with the colliery, how on earth do you propose to fund this scheme of yours? We can barely afford to stay here."

"The funding of her place is already met, Hannah."

"But how?"

"I went to see Browns of Westbridge, the antique dealer—"

Now understanding what was different about the room, through gritted teeth, an irate Hannah sneered:

"How dare you sell some of my family's treasured possessions to fund your—love-child!"

"I have no choice. I do not wish to continue living in this odious environment, and I have my duties as a father to meet."

Reflecting on the situation, Hannah gave out a sigh. *On balance, I suppose eroding our long-term wealth to get rid of the irritating stone in the shoe of my life has to be worth it.*

"So be it," she said with a resigned tone.

"Now go!" he instructed, looking back down at the papers dismissively.

Later that evening, the Harveys gathered for yet another meal in silence.

9

THE PLAN IS REVEALED

The next day, the mood in the house was still dark and foreboding. Mrs Harvey only spoke to her children to berate them for not doing something to her liking. Shrill orders were given to Meg or Sarah. To her husband, she barely uttered a word.

Of late, when her chores were done, Bess had taken to seeking solace in the servants' bedroom, tending to her embroidery. Sarah had kindly donated a scrap of cloth, some needles and coloured yarn to get her started. One evening, in the warm, yellowy glow of the oil lamp, she had given the young girl some basic instruction on how to do the common stitches. Keen to hone this new skill, headstrong as usual, Bess raced ahead. Her handiwork so ragged in places, Sarah told her it needed to be unpicked and redone. Undeterred, she was grateful that reworking the design was delaying her progress; her meagre sewing resources would last that bit longer.

Needing to cut some pretty blue thread to begin another flower, with no scissors to hand, she spun her legs off the bed and crept along towards the kitchen. Always keen to avoid the temper of the lady of the house, she had mastered the art of skulking along, undetected.

She was just about to knock on the half-open door, when she stopped in her tracks, not wanting to interrupt the servants' private conversation.

"I've got something to do, and I am dreading it, Sarah."

"Dreading what?" she replied. "We've been in plenty of tight spots over the years, but we always manage. Come on, tell me—a problem shared and all that—"

Meg took a deep breath, then began.

"Well, I'd popped to Woodborough today, on some errands for Mrs 'arvey, and I bumped into the vicar."

"'ow is the old fellow? 'e looks like a shadow of 'is former self these days. Drawn and weary in the face, if you ask me."

"Aye. 'e wasn't biding too well when I saw 'im, Sarah. 'e was coming back from a meeting with the Guardians—more pauper burials to conduct for 'em apparently—those poor wretched souls."

"That place is beastly. I never want to set foot in it! Whenever I look at my 'ands rubbed raw with housework, I remember that it's better 'ere than in there."

"Quite, Meg. 'e told me one of the folks 'ad only been in the workhouse for a few days before the Lord chose to take 'em. Days. Walked in more or less right as rain, caught the fever and slipped away."

Sarah slowly shook her head in dismay from side to side as she continued.

"Well, the vicar looked bothered about this latest burial, which I found strange. Why talk to me about it? After all, with all the disease there, them weak, sick and old folks, then it's to be expected. 'e must have done loads. The thing is—"

Meg paused to compose herself.

"The thing is, that new intern who departed was Bess's mother. She's been slung in one of those deep, unmarked graves in the workhouse grounds. Seventeen other bodies were already down there, 'e said. It's barbaric what they do to those people. I've 'eard talk the stench is awful, them all rotting away in their coffins before the ground is finally filled in. I don't 'ave the 'eart to tell her. Should we wait a little longer, until she's better settled? It'll break her 'eart learning about her ma's terrible fate, Sarah, I know it will."

Out in the corridor, a distraught Bess raised her arm and hid her eyes in the dark fold of her elbow, then slumped against the wall in despair.

She tried to retain her composure, but her sobs had taken control of her breathing. A loud, unconscious gulp of air alerted the servant girls who had just fallen silent as a mark of respect.

The two women stared at each other, bitterly disappointed the news had been so carelessly divulged to the poor girl.

They picked her up with great affection and swept her into the kitchen. Sat on Sarah's knee, Meg wiped away her tears with the corner of her apron.

"The vicar said it was swift, Bess. She slipped unconscious almost as soon as she'd arrived. She didn't suffer. You 'ave to be grateful for that."

"What's done is done," said Bess, darkly. "I've lost my grandfather and survived. And I never really 'ad a father—well, until now—I am used to being alone."

"Still, she was your mother, Bess," Sarah said, as she took to smoothing her hand over the child's unruly hair to comfort her.

Collecting her composure, Bess announced, "I came to cut this yarn." She unclenched her right hand, revealing a crushed clump of thread, wetted by her tears.

"Right you are, Miss," said Sarah, setting her down and fetching the scissors.

Meg trimmed the tiny ball of yarn into shorter, more manageable pieces, then took her hand and helped the stoic little child back to the bedroom.

"It's a good thing she's as tough as old boots, Sarah. She's taken it very well considering," said Meg on her return.

"That's all well and good, but she can't live on being resilient, Meg. She'll be needing an 'usband to make ends meet."

Bess tried her best to clear her head and focused intently on how she positioned her needle in the square of cloth. Feeling determined, she was in the mood for progress that evening, not unpicking ugly stitching. Besides, the extra concentration required to make an excellent job of it had turned into a good way to silence the secret voices of fear and sadness that kept plaguing her since her arrival at Walton.

Upstairs, her father had finished working in the study and had gone to find Bess to tell her what had been decided. He made his way purposefully downstairs, mentally reviewing his delivery as he walked.

With Meg and Sarah out of earshot, still in the kitchen, he was pleased to find Bess was alone when he entered their bedroom. She turned to look at him and smiled. *Perhaps he's heard about Ma? Be brave, Bess. Don't let him see you saddened about the news.*

Sitting on the edge of her bed, he reached out his right hand as hers let go of the embroidery fabric. With trepidation, she rested her tiny hand on his warm, outstretched palm. He gently laid his other hand on top, giving hers a reassuring, parental squeeze.

"I have some good news, my dearest Bess. I've been speaking to my brother and the lady of the house. We have decided that you should go to boarding school. They will turn you into a fine young woman, and an education will stand you in good stead before you are married."

With Bess's big eyes looking up at him earnestly, his began to sting with emotion. Although proud of his decision, his thoughts were tinged with sadness that she would be leaving Walton Hall for most of her young little life. Mr Harvey thought it best to break his gaze. Looking at the floor, he continued.

"I'm sure you will not take this opportunity for granted. It is a considerable investment for the family. We have made quite a sacrifice to secure it for you."

His grip tightened on her hand to convey this was an offer not to be refused.

Bess was stunned. *Leaving already? I've barely adjusted to departing grandfather's cottage to take up this strange new way of life. My mother is gone. And oh, how I'll miss*

Meg and Sarah. They have been so kind to me. And of course, my father, a man who has taken me on as his own to spare me from the Union. If only I could have seen more of him before being sent away. Mrs Harvey might be angry with him, but I can see he is principled at heart. A fleeting visit at Christmas or Easter will be our only time together. I'd better say something quick else I'll look most ungrateful.

"Why thank you, Mr 'arvey, Sir. I was 'appy being a servant for you, I truly was. Your generosity has taken my tongue. Me, at boarding school, getting an education. Who would 'ave thought it!" she beamed?

She hid her disappointment that the separation would mean she would not have time to learn more about her father. However, it was not her decision to make. *What if he tires of me in my absence? Abandons me?* Equally, she felt a glimmer of delight to be free of the oppressive atmosphere that followed the beastly Mrs Harvey, the big black cloud of doom personified.

Sensing it was perhaps all too much for young Bess to take in, her father kissed her tenderly the forehead then said, "Goodnight. Try and get some rest. You'll be leaving in the morning."

He turned down the oil lamp in her room as a sign she should sleep, knowing full well that she would stay wide awake, the anxiety gnawing at her. He gently closed the door and told Meg and Sarah to be as quiet as dormice when they retired.

In the morning, Bess was gone. It would be many long years until she completed her schooling and could once more reside permanently at Walton Hall.

10

THE ENGAGEMENT PARTY

It was early one Sunday morning when she returned for good. A strong, black horse trotted up the drive of Walton Hall, pulling a muddied carriage. On its roof, was a large wooden chest, firmly strapped down. An anxious Bess looked out of the window, noticing the exterior of the building had barely changed, except the ivy was covering more of the front facade.

She was two hours late, with heavy rain making her travel treacherous along miles and miles of waterlogged and potholed roads. *We will be eating brunch, not breakfast. I'm so late!*

Being away from Walton Hall had enabled the dust to settle in the Harvey household to a certain extent. Her short, infrequent visits like at the holidays had helped her to forge a stronger bond with her siblings, and of course, her father had not forgotten her. She was now very much a daughter, rather than a 'servant' or 'orphan'. The youngest daughter, Nell, had tended to side with her mother in the early days, but thankfully, now saw Bess more like her equal, especially as they were close in age. As to be expected, Mrs Harvey was as cruel as ever in private, but at least had feigned being civil in public during Bess's visits.

She rang the doorbell. Meg and Sarah were delighted to see the beautiful young woman return.

"Look at you, Miss, a fine young lady you are now."

She was grateful that jealousy had not ruined their relationship, and the early kindness and support they showed her had been maintained.

An unusually cheerful Robert Harvey announced:

"Come, let us have some food, you must be starving."

The coachman heaved her luggage from the roof and brought it inside.

Half an hour later, the family gathered in the dining room. The children, now young adults themselves, asked Bess about what her plans were now her school years were behind her. Laid in the middle of the table was a series of eye-catching serving bowls. Under their domed lids, awaited some delicious home-cooked bacon, eggs, sausages, golden-brown toast, to which they all tucked into. Meg poured their tea in the best china cups, starting with Mr Harvey's.

Only one thing was missing—Mrs Harvey.

She'd already excused herself from attending breakfast the day before, saying her sister was ill and requested her presence. In truth, her sister was in fine health. Hannah had faked the need for the overnight visit. She sought Carlyle familial support to help her cope with the impending—permanent—return of her philandering husband's illegitimate child. She still loathed 'that damned girl.'

Bess's late arrival meant Mrs Harvey returned ten minutes after the family began dining. She would be expected to join them.

One by one, the family finished their meal and excused themselves. That left Bess who had stayed to the end to be polite, and the late-arriving Mrs Harvey alone together. The atmosphere was suffocating.

Hannah breathed deeply through her nose, then broke the silence.

> "You may think you have an air of respectability now you've been to boarding school, dearest child," she taunted, "But I will always remember where you truly came from. You cannot hide that from me. I will make sure you know your place."

Bess set down her cup and left, saying nothing. She'd learned over the years that it was the best way to manage the frosty situation.

She breezed along the hallway and upstairs to her room, her own bedroom, not the shared servants' quarters where she used to stay when she arrived all those years ago.

She opened up the lid of her heavy travelling chest and took out the keepsake brooch that her mother gave her and gripped it tightly. What she would give to see her darling mother now, a mother who always looked after her, despite her meagre resources and cruel hardships life had seen to bestow upon her. There was still a glowing warmth in her heart for her.

A convenient way to escape the oppressive home environment was to attend church. The afternoon service provided a timely reason to be absent. If she took the route down the lane, past the boating lake to Woodborough, she could be away for longer still. It was a fantastic opportunity to relax in the fresh air, taking in the beauty of the hedgerows and the sound of the countryside. She always felt at peace in her own company. She knew one person she could constantly rely on was herself.

The long path, of course, also passed close to the gamekeeper's cottage. She'd always remembered Harry for his kindness, helping her when he found her battered and bleeding after her boathouse ordeal. She had enjoyed spending glorious, but fleeting, moments with him when she was home from school for the holidays. With hope in her heart, she walked along the stony surface of the lane, lifting her skirts just a little to keep them out of the occasional puddle.

She was to be lucky! In the distance was Harry, now twenty-four. She noticed his outdoor life kept him trim and muscular. No longer a child, Bess felt her feelings change towards him over the years, and she was now even more drawn to him than before.

He waved as he saw her, and strode over with a spring to his step.

"Why Miss Harvey, it's you," he said surprised. He had not expected her back, thinking term-time had a couple more weeks left to run.

She looked over to see him and felt her heart leap. It soon crashed back down though as she saw a young woman about Harry's age outside the cottage washing clothes in a bucket. She had been pushing them around with purpose, with a long wooden dolly, then pegging them out, even his undergarments. As the woman raised her arms up, Bess could see a wedding ring glinting on her left hand.

"May I walk with you a while, Miss. There's lots of news to tell you."

I bet there is. Like that woman being your wife, perhaps? That's quite a revelation.

"Yes, you can, Harry. I always delight in your stories about the estate." She hoped her face hadn't betrayed her angst. She was sure Harry's news would involve the woman.

She had dreamed of telling him she was back for good, maybe not on the day itself but soon. Now that idea was ruined. She did her best to keep her disappointment to herself.

Having grown accustomed to hiding his feelings too, Harry's restless heart skipped a beat, delighted to think that he would see Bess more regularly now her schooling was over. As a recluse, working long hours patrolling the estate alone, he had still not found himself a wife. Besides, the cottage he lived in was not the place to raise a family. It was far too small, and there were lots of dangers around the home, mantraps, and guns and the like, to deal with any nuisance poachers. Plus, his meagre earnings were too slender to fund a family. Lord Hamilton was not known for his generosity towards his staff.

Thankfully though, as part of his tenure on the estate, one of the lord's servant girls was instructed to help on the sabbath to keep the place clean. It's true Harry Sutherland was a man used to living off the land, relying on his wits. He wasn't too taken with comfort. Still, he was human, and his heart did yearn for a wife to warm him on cold winter nights.

Bess couldn't help herself but stare at him. He was just as handsome in profile, as he was when she looked directly at him. Fortunately, Harry was focusing on looking ahead and didn't notice her transfixed expression.

Suddenly Bess lost her footing, failing to notice a pothole in the lane. Her toes were stubbed, and her ankle bent over awkwardly as her leg suddenly gave way. Harry rushed to hold her. The pain in her ankle was searing, but she didn't care. The way she felt as he held her made her forget all about it. There was an undeniable bond between them. Two lone souls united.

Seconds later, the tenderness was replaced with awkwardness and the instant she was steady on her feet, he let go. Neither of them knew what to make of the encounter; him secretly besotted unable to tell her how he felt, and Bess trying not to yearn for her 'married' beau.

Harry quickly turned the conversation to life in Woodborough.

"I hear your sister, young Miss Harriet, is soon to be married?"

"Yes, that's one of the reasons I've come back a little earlier than planned. We are to have a big party this evening."

"It'll be your turn, soon, Bess," Harry added, trying to gauge her response at the subtle hint he was interested in her in that way.

"Yes, I am sure. Mr Harvey has plans for us all, no doubt," she replied distantly, wondering why Harry wasn't mentioning how he got married. *Should I ask him, or is that too presumptuous?*

They found themselves almost at the end of the lane between Hamilton House and Walton Hall.

"Well, I'd better be getting back," said Harry, his cottage in the distance, still with the woman in view.

"Thanks for the company Harry, and catching me from falling. Meg and Sarah would have had a lot of trouble cleaning the mud out of my dress."

"T'was nothin' Miss Harvey. You take care now—" he said, disappearing along a smaller path through the woodland.

Bess continued her stroll to the church service, her thoughts instinctively returning to the delicious moment where he had caught her. *Why am I like a moth to a flame when it comes to Harry Sutherland? Now what? Harry is married, sure of his future. I am still adrift. I suppose people might see me as an accomplished woman, having been away to school. But at heart, I am still a shepherd's granddaughter. Besides, living in a beautiful hall comes to nought if you have a heartless husband. I would not wish to swap places with a lady in Mrs Harvey's predicament. A loveless marriage. The shame of being 'inadequate' for her spouse. The betrayal, selfishness, defeat and lies. None of it your own making. Except for being unwelcoming in bed? Perhaps that was during her pregnancies? I am close in age to the others, I suppose.*

After the service, she returned back to Walton Hall, this time keen to avoid encountering Harry 'the husband' Sutherland along the way. She took the other route back to Walton. She couldn't face seeing him after the shocking discovery of the woman. It hurt too much. Once again, preferring to keep herself busy, she continued with some needlework she had started at boarding school; the colourful design was a tapestry of the hall. It was for Sarah and Meg to brighten the drab walls of their bedroom.

That evening's family gathering was to be the biggest one the Harveys and their wider family had seen for some time. The eldest daughter, Harriet, had accepted the hand in marriage of a local clerk, William, who worked as an accountant for his father, Mr Burridge. The plan was to create a lavish affair, so no one suspected that the colliery was still struggling at times, thus boosting the perceived 'eligibility' of Richard, Nell and Bess.

The servants were busy preparing the house, tidying, cleaning and decorating rooms with fresh flowers, ready for the night's planned festivities. After that, they returned to the kitchen to cook the food. They made a sterling job of eking out the ingredients without it looking like they were cutting corners. Despite their meagre budget, thanks to the servants having good relationships with the shop owners in Woodborough, they were able to get good quality food that was in season at reasonable prices.

With everyone focusing on the party ahead, a rare, joyous atmosphere filled Walton Hall.

Bess heard a knock at her door. Harriet's voice wafted through.

> "Can you help me with my dress? It is a new one, especially for this evening. The buttons are so awkward for me to do up."

Bess leapt from her bed and went to her sister's aid. As she helped Harriet with the fastenings, Nell, helped with the final touches to her already perfectly coiffured hair. Afterwards, the two youngest girls left to get changed into their outfits, leaving a nervous, but radiant Harriet to her thoughts.

At seven-thirty, the first of the guests began to arrive, and a happy hubbub from the assembled throng filled the air.

Nell and Bess walked downstairs in their most elegant dresses, synchronising each step as they went. They were keen to see who had been invited; the attendees had been decided by Mr and Mrs Harvey alone. They had both tried to second-guess which eligible bachelors might have been invited as potential suitors.

The great and the good from Woodborough, along with many of the Harvey clan, and the Carlyles from Hannah's side were engaged in polite conversation. The wine flowed freely, and burgeoning plates of food were distributed amongst the partygoers.

Feeling less inhibited with a little wine in her belly, Bess confessed to Nell she was attracted to someone, Hannah's nephew. Fred Carlyle. *He is second-best to Harry Sutherland of course, couldn't hold a candle to him, but at least he is unattached.* After all the investment and sacrifice her father had made for her, as a colliery owner's daughter, she would be expected to be betrothed to a man of means.

"Come! Let this party begin! Please join me for some music!" announced Mr Harvey, and signalled to the quartet assembled in one corner of the spacious parlour to begin playing a lively jig.

Earlier in the day, the larger pieces of furniture had been heaved to the side of the room, and the smaller, delicate items safely stored in the servants' quarters.

A group of guests took their partners, and began their twirling steps and skipped under the raised arms of their fellow dancers.

The two young girls stood politely at the side of the room, assessing the attendees for a likeable young man to dance with, with Bess in particular, following Fred Carlyle round the parlour. Her heart was in her mouth. Fred too had the same strong features as the gamekeeper and was easily as tall. She could feel the blood flushing her face with embarrassment, just like it had in the afternoon after she had stumbled in the lane, and Harry had caught her. She'd spent very little time in male company in her lifetime so far, except for her brother and father, since she attended an all-girls' school. Thanks to her love of reading, she knew how to approach men in theory, should the opportunity present itself, but became tongue-tied in real life.

At last at the party, where polite conversation with several men in one evening was acceptable, she had an opportunity to work on her technique.

Mr Harvey looked across at his two daughters, becoming increasingly irritated they seemed to be endlessly talking to each other and not the carefully curated guests. The party had cost a small fortune, and yet, his girls seemed more eager to talk to each other, something they could do for free at any time. *It is high time they started looking for husbands.*

As the last few bars of the song were played, Richard shouted to Robert:

"What say you? We have a jig, father? Something even livelier!"

"Yes, I agree," his father roared doing his best to look carefree and full of life.

He clapped his hands to signal a change in tempo, and the guests began another country dance, twisting and turning their way around the parlour's makeshift dance floor. Robert was pleased his suggestion had worked as he saw his guests swap dance partners, every few bars.

But still, his two daughters were focused on each other, giggling nervously behind their hands, whispering. Bess's gaze kept locking onto Fred Carlyle as he danced around the room. Still, she was too scared to approach him, despite the many years of dancing practice at school. *'Please let my powder cover up my embarrassment if he comes over'*, she prayed, feeling her face redden.

Losing patience inside, but remaining composed to onlookers, Robert Harvey made sure he would be standing right beside them when the jig ended, so he could push the girls onto the dance floor; force them to mingle with the other guests. *How am I supposed to find them husbands if they insist on excluding themselves from the festivities? They will be happy old maids if I am not careful.*

"Let's have another, this time with my lovely daughters taking part."

A faint ripple of welcoming polite applause rang out. He took them both by the wrist, his tight grip indicating his displeasure at their voluntary exclusion from the party guests.

Filled with joy and fear, Bess found herself partnered with Fred Carlyle. Taking the lead, he turned to face her, placing his hand on her waist, and she hers on his shoulder. The fingers of their other hands entwined, and they were off spiralling around the room. *Look, he's smiling.* Bess glanced up at her handsome dance partner, utterly captivated. Eager not to look too obvious with her affections, she looked over his shoulder, trying to see who Nell had been partnered with. As she did so, she lost concentration, and she stepped on her dance partner's toes, then apologised profusely. He gave no clue as to whether he was displeased, or forgiving. He seemed somewhat distant. *Is that a good or a bad thing?*

She felt some eyes following her; her father's. He was talking to a man from Woodborough, but the chap in question didn't seem to be paying that much attention to him. *He's not even looking at my father? How rude.*

She hoped her choice of dance partner would please Robert Harvey. After all, his wife's family were comfortably off, and so Fred Carlyle was clearly a suitable prospect.

As the song petered out, the smile on Fred's face evaporated, much to Bess's disappointment. She had hoped the next dance would be theirs too. She put a brave face on, regardless, and hoped her eyes hinted that she would like to continue.

> "Do not smile at me, Madam. I know who you truly are. Your father might be able to fool the locals, that you are but an orphan, but I know you still have a parent, and that parent is him. My Aunt Hannah has explained everything to me. You are his illegitimate child after him carrying on with that harlot from the colliery. Nothing but a mongrel, despite all that schooling."

The words stung poor Bess, her poor heart breaking into more pieces as it was struck with each wicked phrase.

As the music started up again, Fred continued with his tirade against her, his ugly comments delivered like an actor would speak the polished lines of a play, with the playwright being her nemesis, Hannah Harvey.

> "I want a wholesome and good wife, who comes from a good family. Not a cuckoo, that's tried to sneak into the nest, with its selfish attitude and lazy demeanour. Rising to the top at the expense of others."

At these last words, Bess was tipped over the edge, her rage finally boiling over.

"I am no such thing, Sir. My mother was in desperate straits when my grandfather died. She had no choice but to bring me here, rather than take me to the workhouse to rot away, and for that, I am grateful. I was a mere child. It was her decision. I am no parasite, Mr Carlyle." She hissed in his ear.

"You are wasting your time looking for a husband here, my girl. I shall make sure all the eligible Harveys and Carlyles know your true background. My uncle has done nothing but leech off my family. He, like you, is a loafer and a failure, always going cap in hand to ask for money when that colliery of his runs into trouble."

As they danced around the room, Bess did her best to let the criticism fall on deaf ears. *Why is this song so long? I am tired of enduring these insults.*

She looked to her father, still talking to the same man, but at least now he was facing him. Her dance partner, Fred Carlyle, showed no signs of stopping talking either.

"I intend to ask the hand in marriage of a respectable young lady of a fine pedigree. Her father is a local gentleman, a skilled engineer and inventor, whose cotton is sought after throughout the Empire. His daughter will be fitting to my status, not a ragged, unwanted love-child like you."

Mercifully, the musicians playing slowed and quietened. They were taking a short interlude. Bess dropped her arms and furiously turned her back on the hateful nephew. Leaving the parlour, grabbing a glass of wine as she left, she returned to her room for a few moments to gather her thoughts. She took out her mother's brooch and stroked the delicate design.

I understand you did what was best for me, but I fear I will never really be accepted by most of these well-to-do folks. They always see the urchin in me, the lost little girl you abandoned— deposited—here all those years ago. It is a stain that will not wash out.

Knowing her absence would irk her father, she finished the wine in a few large gulps, hoping the warm, fruity liquid would numb her sense of regret. *I hate being ungrateful for the opportunity my lovely mother had bravely chosen for me, but sometimes, I just wish my life was as it should have been. How I wish I could be with Harry now. Be his wife. He understands me, but that is an impossibility now.*

All she could do was hold her mother's brooch for a few more seconds and wait for calmer thoughts to be restored, though, how long it might take to soothe her heartache was unknown.

Downstairs, Robert Harvey had managed to introduce Nell to the son of a man who owned an engineering company, whom he thought might be a suitor for her. *But where is Bess? That ungrateful child!* He was seething, and his anger worsened the longer Bess was missing.

Earlier in the day, Robert and Hannah had sat down to-gether to discuss their financial situation, which was still somewhat precarious. The expensive party had burned a large hole in their budget, but they had agreed window-dressing their situation, by throwing a lavish party was the best way to convince others they were flourishing.

"I do not need to stress how important it is that we find husbands and a wife for these children of ours." he'd said. "All of them," he added before Hannah could rule Bess out of the equation. Despite our differences, Hannah, we must pull together, and present a united happy front to the outside world. I believe our youngest Nell should marry someone close to your family. I understand that your eldest nephew, Fred plans to be betrothed to that cotton mill owner's daughter, and therefore he is not available."

"That is correct," Hannah confirmed. "Perhaps we could consider his younger brother, Jonathan. He seems to be thriving with his career as a railway engineer."

"Yes, let's make sure they are properly introduced this evening. I feel that Bess is better matched to an older gentleman. Someone who has perhaps been married before. A widower who will have different—more flexible—expectations of a suitable wife. I have somebody in mind, one of my advisors at the colliery, Mr Mortimer. I believe he is a good match. He will be able to support her, given that we have little in the way of money to give her to help them set up their household. That just leaves our son. He seems so preoccupied with helping with the colliery. He hasn't had time to court anyone. He's certainly not mentioned anyone that may have taken his eye. That will need some more thought."

"I shall ponder on that, Robert," said Hannah, being uncharacteristically obliging.

"Clearly, marrying our eldest daughter to an accountant is a good decision. It is an honest and solid profession and offers skills that will always be in demand, no matter what industry. And of course, having access to financial advice that we can trust and will remain within these four walls, cannot be underestimated. Some more strong alliances with other successful families will be our making, Hannah."

Now, with the party in full swing, Robert Harvey frequently smiled at Hannah, and in earshot of as many people as possible loudly praised her for being such a wonderful wife, and how lucky they were to have such a happy, prosperous home. The wine flowed. The food followed in a seemingly inexhaustible supply. Secretly, he was fuming though, wondering where on earth Bess had got to.

11

THE UNEXPLAINED ABSENCE

In his quest to marry off his children, Robert had seen fit to invite the local doctor, Dr Croft, the solicitor, Mr Mortimer, and several industrialists with plenty of young sons and daughters in the prime of life, as well as their own wider families. Throughout the party, Hannah had to call on all her strength to present a united front with her husband. The strain of Bess coming back to live at the house full-time weighed heavily upon her. She put on a brave face in public to appease Robert.

On Bess's eventual return to the parlour, Robert Harvey politely excused himself and made his way over to her. He grabbed her discreetly but roughly around the arm, signalling his displeasure at her disappearance.

"I have someone you should meet."

He paced her towards the large parlour doors opening onto the courtyard outside. He loosened his grip and told her under his breath to look approachable. Bess was quite startled by his harshness, something usually reserved for his wife. A group of three well-dressed men, two younger and one older, stood by the doorway, earnestly discussing a business matter. Knowing these may be suiters, Bess decided the younger, fair-haired man on the left was her favourite.

"My dear. Let me introduce you to Mr Mortimer— Edward Mortimer. He's my company solicitor. He looks after all of our commercial contracts at the colliery. He's a very clever man."

"Pleased to make your acquaintance, Mr Mortimer. Miss Bess Harvey," she said, reaching out a hand to the oldest, stoutest and ugliest of the three men by far.

Robert continued to eulogise about Edward. All Bess could see was his ugliness. His malmsey nose was bright red, presumably from years of drinking. His saggy, heavy-lidded eyes, with unsightly bags underneath them, looked more like slits. His face was severely pock-marked. *Please not the lingering aftermath of some sort of pox?* He had done his best to hide the visible craters with the bushy, brown muttonchop sideburns tinged with grey, that cloaked his round, fat face, but had failed in his endeavours—the ugliness shone through regardless.

His waistcoat buttons struggled to contain his portly physique within the taut fabric. He clearly had an office job, rather than the frame typical of a strong young man who worked on the land.

Keen to talk to the eligible, well-educated young woman in front of him, Edward Mortimer led Bess outside into the courtyard, lighting a cigar as he walked. He puffed on it furiously in between the first awkward, stilted sentences they exchanged, looking more like a barrel-chested, burly steam train cloaked in smoke than a man. Even though they were outside, the air reeked of the pungent tobacco.

Bess plucked up the courage to ask a personal question.

"Are you here with your wife, Mr Mortimer?"

"I'm afraid not," he replied.

His face saddened, and his eyes fell to the floor.

"I've not been lucky in love, Miss Harvey. I've had two wives, and both of them God chose to take from me in childbirth. None of the children survived either. I'm now alone."

At that point, her worst fears were confirmed. Her father had clearly decided this unsightly, older fellow as a suitable husband for her. After all, solicitors earned a good income, and his skills were an asset to the colliery, just like Harriet's intended, the accountant William Burridge.

Mr Mortimer, on the other hand, was smitten with the girl. She was a vision of loveliness. The fresh, ivory-white skin on her face was framed by a few flowing tresses of hair, and the bulk of it tamed and gathered at the nape of her shapely neck with a pretty red ribbon. She was a vision of beauty. Her shapely outline was clearly visible as she wore her tight-fitting off-the-shoulder dress with a scooped neck. *She is a manifestation of heaven on earth.*

Despite his best efforts, Edward failed to build any rapport with Bess. He sensed she was repulsed. However, her father had confided to him that he would see to them marrying. His sense of irritation was rising, annoyed his time was being wasted. *Obviously, he has not spoken to his daughter about the matter!*

Mr Mortimer collected two glasses of wine in a last attempt to shake off Bess's disgust. *Can she not see that I am a man of means? I can guarantee her much more security than a young upstart of a man, clinging to his father's wallet for protection.* Bess didn't seem to want her wine, so he drank it down in one big gulp.

Eager to see what progress was being made by Mr Mortimer, Robert Harvey came out to the courtyard, open-armed and smiling. Witnessing the meeting had a frosty air to it, he lowered his arms, and his look became more steely. Bess knew that was a look of disappointment, caused by her; disappointment that would not be tolerated. Bess's heart sank, for she knew from bitter experience what disobeying an implicit order from her father could entail. *My stepmother is the walking embodiment of that.*

Robert took control of the situation and informed Mr Mortimer he wanted a word in private with his daughter.

"Of course, my good fellow. I need to fill my glass." He replied as he turned to go inside, looking a little unsteady on his feet after all the drink he'd had in the past half hour.

Mr Harvey did his customary grab of her arm, digging his thumb into her elbow much more aggressively this time.

"May I remind you, dearest daughter that you are a drain on this household and you have been a drain on this household since I took you in. I have shown you a lot of generosity. I've been kind to you. I've paid for your schooling. It is now time for you to do something for me. I suggest you find something in common with Mr Mortimer before I force you to have something in common with him."

Her father went to collect her intended suitor and suggested they both go out to the courtyard again. Nightfall was starting to chill the air, and everyone had come inside. Out there, they could talk privately.

Almost in tears, reluctantly, she stepped outside. She didn't know what she was going to talk to him about and hoped that something would come to mind. She let the mountain of a man in front of her lead the conversation. It seemed the safest thing to do. Inside she panicked but felt at least if she were civil now, she wouldn't incur more of her father's disappointment. It was getting late, and the guests would be going home soon. She just had to delay Mr Mortimer's advances a little longer. In the meantime, she did her best to be welcoming.

Fifteen minutes later, Edward came back inside, having made his assessment, and shared it with Bess's father.

"Your Bess oozes charm and possesses a wild young heart. She is resilient. Feisty even. Ripe for providing me with a healthy child too. She is someone who could bring happiness to my later years, as well as tend and care for me."

"I'm very pleased to hear that my good fellow. Why don't you come back next week, and we shall announce your engagement? I shall talk to her and explain that you are a good gentleman who runs a successful business and would be an excellent suitor for her. She will be in no doubt what is expected of her, I assure you."

In their eagerness to discuss their arrangement, Robert and Edward had overlooked Bess's whereabouts. In the darkness, she had sneaked back into the house via the servants' entrance, desperate to keep out of the parlour.

In the hallway, she met Nell and asked how her evening was going.

"Oh, it's been awful Bess. Mother introduced me to the most boring of fellows, Fred's brother, Jonathan. He's an engineer. Works in the railways. He only seemed to talk about himself and never listened to what I had to say. I think they see him as husband material. The thought of a lifetime with him fills me with dread. It will be so terribly, terribly dull."

"At least he is handsome, my dear sister," lamented Bess. "Father has shown his hand about his plans for me. He has chubby, red-faced Mr Mortimer in his sights as my future husband."

"Mr Mortimer? But he's—" said Nell, unable to complete the sentence, understandably shocked that a portly, pock-marked man twice her age, and with two marriages behind him already was considered an eligible candidate for her sweet and delicate sister.

"Quite!" replied a horrified Bess.

Earlier in the day, the two girls had hoped they would be introduced to handsome, eligible suitors, letting the idea of a romantic match run away with them, clouding their judgement. It seemed that their parents had settled on these two men, purely on the strength of beneficial business alliances for the family. It was the usual way of things, after all. Nell added:

"I think they want me to marry him quickly. Father said he is to come to the house next week to ask for my hand in marriage. I cannot believe how fast the matter is progressing."

The hallway clock's hands were pointing towards midnight. The last of the partygoers were beginning to leave.

Mr and Mrs Harvey were thanking them for visiting, making sure Meg and Sarah brought the right person the right coat. Mr Mortimer and young Mr Jonathan Carlyle were two of the last to leave. The girls overheard their father invite them to visit again in the week. Their hearts sank.

The following week, as planned the two gentlemen took up their invites to visit Walton Hall, with Mr Carlyle the first of the two to appear in the parlour.

Nell capitulated immediately. Utterly unable to go against her parent's wishes, she agreed to the engagement. She wouldn't be the first woman forced to learn to love her future husband. *At least 'Mr Boring' has money, and he looks charming. Compared with Bess's fate, I think I have fared better.*

The day after, the bulky figure of Mr Mortimer lumbered up the driveway, his body almost as wide as the door. The doorbell rang, then Meg answered and escorted him to the parlour, where Bess and Mr and Mrs Harvey were waiting.

A splendid display of afternoon tea cakes was on a silver trolley, which was served in silence by Sarah, along with a cup of tea each. The conversation was stilted and awkward until Sarah left, closing the door behind her discreetly.

With the welcoming formalities out of the way, Mr Harvey suggested that Bess and Mr Mortimer should take in some of the glorious fresh air and sunshine outside, giving the solicitor his cue to propose.

Bess's heart sank, but she had no choice but to agree to the suggestion. *Think, Bess, think. You just can't marry this man. There has to be a better fellow in father's social circle.*

As they strolled along the gravel pathway, past the glorious flowerbeds, with the marigolds and black-eyed susans dancing in the breeze, Bess did her best to stick to pleasantries. She discussed the weather and the beauty of the flowers, but it was in vain. She couldn't avoid the inevitable.

Mr Mortimer stepped a couple of paces ahead quickly and blocked her route forward. He took her hands in his, and through his fat, puffy eyes stared into hers.

"Bess Harvey, would you do me the honour of becoming my wife?"

She looked at him, bit her lip and fought back some tears, trapped between obligation, a lack of money and a lack of choice. Duty, expectation, tradition, custom, it all conspired against her, robbing her of any chance of expressing her free will.

Bess paused, frozen with dread.

A million thoughts flitted through her head. She had known this moment was coming since the party and had planned out how to handle it. She would accept, looking to the good in kindly, but repellent Mr Mortimer. The disappointment to her father if she rejected the request would be unbearable.

But, when the moment came to agree, the words stuck in her throat. The resilient spirit of her long-departed mother seemed to flow within her. Bess's independent, unorthodox streak could not be suppressed yet. *I have started life from nothing, and I could do it again.*

Doing the best to spare his feelings, but failing, she blurted out:

> "No, Mr Mortimer, I am sorry but I will not! I've only just left school. I am but a young girl. I'm not worthy of a fine older man of substance like you—"

Tears stung her eyes as she picked up her skirts and ran, knowing the portly Mr Mortimer would struggle to catch up to her. She headed out towards the boathouse at the far end of the garden. Anywhere was better than being next to her 'intended' or her soon-to-be dismayed father.

Edward Mortimer fumed, his red face reddening further. He was apoplectic. He turned on his heels, feeling his nose had been pushed rudely out of joint. *How dare she spurn me? How dare that rotter Harvey humiliate me? He has had several days to make her see sense!*

He marched into the parlour, demanding the servants bring his hat and coat. A stunned Mr and Mrs Harvey shared his anger. Nothing they could say could ease Mortimer's rage or embarrassment.

"It's a good job I can afford servants to look after my household, Mr Harvey, for your girl thinks she is too good for me," he yelled, furiously fighting to get his fat arms in his coat sleeves.

He pulled his hat on firmly and stormed out of the room, with Meg struggling to keep up with him to open the front door.

"But Edward—" Robert shouted after him, trying to apologise for his daughter's feckless, ungrateful behaviour, but it was pointless. Mr Mortimer was halfway down the drive already.

A furious Robert Harvey poured a large whiskey and stormed off upstairs to his study, bounding up two steps at a time. The last thing he needed was a tongue-lashing from his wife, full to the brim with 'I told you so' comments about Bess.

He sat behind his desk, his finger tracing around the top of the glass in an attempt to calm down. He wondered how on earth to discipline his wayward daughter. He feared an infernal rage building where he would give her a good walloping to teach her some manners. *Sometimes a man's fists are the only way to communicate. The shame she seems able to bring on this family is without limit.*

Around an hour later, he heard Bess's door give its distinct creak as she tried to slip back to her room. The weather had turned nasty outside. Rain lashed at the windows of Walton Hall, tumbling from a steely grey sky.

In a fit of rage, as he stood up, he thrust the desk chair away with the back of his knees, finding himself rigid like a soldier ordered to stand to attention.

Bess locked the door behind her, and her father hammered on it with his fists, the stinging sensation serving to make him even more incensed. He could hear Bess sobbing in terror between the bangs on the door. *Good. She will learn not to disobey me.*

"Open this door, now!" he ordered, not in a mood to be challenged by her childish antics.

"Come out!"

Nothing happened, except the sobbing was a little quieter, or maybe he was becoming numb to it. Nothing was going to stop him teaching his disappointing daughter a lesson.

"Come out now. You have some explaining to do. How dare you bring shame to the family again. Mr Mortimer is a fine man who does excellent work for me at the colliery. He has the means to take good care of you. He would provide for you in your every need, and yet you snubbed him, treating him worse than a convict awaiting transportation."

His thoughts turned to the family's finances and the cost of his eldest daughter's forthcoming wedding.

"Perhaps Mrs Harvey was right all along. She saw through your selfishness. I will have to find you another good man that will take you off my hands. If you do not accept, I will cast you out of this house. You will be dead to me. Do you understand?"

"Do you?" he bellowed, giving her locked door two hearty kicks in frustration at the same time.

Robert Harvey felt like he was spinning plates on a pole, like a cheap circus entertainer. Four plates represented his adult children who still lived at home, his bitter wife was another plate, and the last one, wobbling precariously, was the colliery.

He was not scared of responsibility. He had a deep sense of obligation. But there were limits, and he did not appreciate his children making life tougher still.

Hearing nothing further from Bess, he decided to cut his losses and return to his whiskey, which unlike others in the house, could be relied upon to act in his best interests.

12

THE TROUBLE AT THE MINE

The next day, Robert Harvey had to turn his attention back to the mine. Things had been running more smoothly in the last few years, thanks to his brother's guiding hand, but another flood after the heavy rain of late had caused chaos.

Thankfully, no lives were lost, but the men were becoming more militant, feeling that the Harvey's were paying scant regard to their safety. Of course, they knew that mining was a risky business. That was why hewing skills were paid more money than other general labouring. Death could greet them at any time. But they weren't prepared to take unnecessary risks when they knew other mines in the area were upgrading their operations to meet with the latest regulations. The labour movement and workers' rights were starting to take hold in the industry. The fledgling collections of workers gave the miners a voice. Together, they felt Mr Harvey would listen to their grievances and make amends. He did seem a fair man—once his own needs were met.

On his arrival at the colliery, there was an angry scuffle, with the men trying to get a glimpse of him, so they could express their frustration personally.

As he left his carriage, he stood on its step, high above the men, and shouted he was meeting with his brother that day, to discuss how to deal with grievances about the flood and how they could be prevented in future. At that, thankfully, the men started to disperse, but only after their unelected spokesman, John Simkins had handed Robert Harvey a long letter detailing all their concerns.

Hearing the kerfuffle outside, David Harvey came to the door of the main office building and waited for his brother to step inside, whence they entered into an in-depth discussion. They were not to be seen for another three hours.

Once his work there was done, David left, and his best underlooker and chief engineer, Charles Falbrook stayed to flesh out the plan to install a more powerful water pump to deal with the flooding. He and Robert Harvey reviewed the solution and began costing the changes required. Cleverly, David had suggested a short-term lease for pumping equipment rather than buying it outright, which was very welcome for the cash-strapped colliery owner.

Over the past few weeks, some of the surface workers, unbeknown to Mr Harvey had commenced some dubious working practices, connecting several bits of rolling stock together with whatever chain was to hand as a makeshift coupling. They wanted to cut down the to-ing and fro-ing and be more efficient. Being paid by the ton produced, cutting corners with safety to speed production and boost pay packets was tempting, and overtook their sense of right and wrong.

The men had also laid some lengths of spare track and sleepers up and over a steep, barely navigable slope to take a more direct route up to the mainline railway depot. Lacking an engine, with a team of four horses, they dragged the hefty, fully laden metal rolling stock from the mineshaft to the railway terminus, avoiding the flatter, winding route that the plethora of smaller wooden carts drawn by single horses used to take

Charles looked out to double-check where the pumping gear housing needed to be installed. After making his decision, he turned his back on the window and began to elaborate on his idea.

He was so engrossed in the finer details of the plan that he hadn't noticed one of the fully laden wagons had broken loose from its substandard coupling to the horses. It glided effortlessly and speedily down the track like a gung-ho child slides on a sledge in winter. It careered, murderously, into the four shire horses towing the next load with a gruesome crunch. Now unstoppable, the hefty weight of the two overfilled, gore-splattered wagons thundered down the track at a furious pace.

The dook runners and pony putters responsible for moving the wagons above ground shouted and waved, running after the heavy cargo, seeing it was going to come off the end of the track and slide along the smooth, thick flagstones and hit the office.

Their efforts were in vain, the wind carried their voices, and besides the two men inside were engrossed. They had finally seen a solution to the latest of the mine's woes.

Paralysed with the breathlessness that comes with running too far too fast, the horrified workers looked on as the wagons smashed into the small, white-washed, stone office. The walls tumbled down like a breeze takes out a house of cards. There had been a direct hit at a weaker spot, between a large glass window and the main door.

With an ominous crash, the building began to collapse. To the onlookers, it seemed to be in slow-motion as it caved in. With a loud shudder, the walls crumbled. The roof beams were snapped like matches. Unsupported, the slate tiles fell in. A column of dust was all that remained of the substantial chimney breast that had served to vent a fireplace on each floor.

The men ran as fast as they could to the ruined office, with the horror of the sight giving them new vigour. Time was of the essence. They needed to free the men quickly if they were to have any hope of survival.

They had last been seen at the upstairs window, so there was at least some slight hope they had survived. *Downstairs, they would surely have been lost under the weight of the fallen masonry?* Stone by stone, plank by plank, slate by slate, the rubble was removed. The men formed long chains passing the debris from hand-to-hand like firemen would pass buckets.

"'Ere. 'Ere. Quick! I can see an 'and pokin' out." yelled Simkins.

Three men rushed to join him, trying to guess where the man's body would be, doing their best not to add their weight to his burden.

The arm was covered in dust. As both men had worn sombre dark suits, it was not clear who they had found first. The men dug feverishly with their bare hands, taking the stone off the battered body beneath. Within a minute, they knew who it was. It was Charles Falbrook, dead as dead can be.

Four of the men took a battered limb each, and carefully carried the body to a grassy piece of land and laid him down, covering his body with their jackets partly for the sake of decorum and partly to hide the fearful bloodied sight, so as not to frighten the younger lads looking on.

The men not directly involved with the rescue took their hats off as a mark of respect as the corpse was removed.

"They must have been close together, lads. Keep looking," ordered Simkins.

The frantic men carried on daisy-chaining the rubble to the sides of the collapsed heap of building.

With more stone out of the way, they saw the corner where Mr Harvey kept his desk. With some more hefty digging, they found some flat, splintered wood. The writing bureau had survived the worst of the blow.

"He might have had time to shelter underneath it?" yelled Billy Woodward, one of the young pit men.

Excavating the dented, collapsed desk, the men heaved it up enough to look underneath.

"'e's there, lads. I think I 'eard a faint groan. Come on, let's get 'im out o' there."

As the desk was removed, they saw a blinking, battered Robert Harvey miraculously still alive. The thick wood seemed to have offered some protection to his head and chest, but the rest of his body had been badly crushed by the fallen stonework.

"The Lord's seen fit to spare 'im!" yelled Billy.

As the other men retrieved their employer, Billy ran off and leapt onto a lone pit pony and galloped off, bareback riding, as fast as he could to Woodborough to fetch the doctor.

Presently, Doctor Croft appeared, charging along in his carriage, the horse pulling it at top speed, with the pit lad following close behind, barely hanging onto the pony. It was a miracle the coach didn't overturn as it took the final bend to the site of the accident.

On seeing the arrival of help, the rescuers were at fever pitch, yelling to the doctor to come over immediately.

Robert Harvey was now unresponsive.

In silence, the doctor performed a rapid assessment of his patient. With the help of a small mirror under the nostrils, there was proof the colliery owner was still breathing—just. *He's fractured his upper arm, judging by how it's bent like that, but thankfully, his head seems to have been spared the worst of the damage. The full extent of his injuries will have to be assessed later. This is not the place to conduct a thorough examination.*

With his skin so bloodied and dust-covered, it was hard to see the precise scale of the wounds. The main priority was to get him somewhere safe and warm before nightfall.

The men formed a make-shift stretcher out of one of the internal doors they salvaged from the rubble and carried their lifeless employer to a long flat-bed cart, in preparation to take him to Walton Hall, where the doctor could tend to him more effectively. Judging by his solemn demeanour, the physician didn't think his patient would last the night.

There are no other obvious deformities in his limbs, but worryingly his abdomen felt quite firm to the touch, and

Doctor Croft was concerned that Mr Harvey might have sustained severe internal injuries.

Sat alongside his patient, in case he regained consciousness or, God forbid, deteriorated further en route, the physician prayed the rain clouds hanging heavy in the sky showed some mercy for this poor, wounded man. Behind, the doctor's carriage clattered along, with four burly banksmen squashed inside, to help unload Mr Harvey on his arrival. The convoy made its way at breakneck speed back to Walton Hall.

Mercifully, Robert Harvey survived the journey, although panic struck in the household as the convoy arrived.

The four labourers took the stretcher upstairs, as carefully as they could take a limp lump of a man sliding about, tethered to a door. They transferred the patient to his bedroom. The pain from the repeated jolting caused the poor man to regain consciousness.

"What is wrong with him?" screamed Mrs Harvey, on the verge of collapse with the dread of the sight.

Young Richard Harvey stepped up to take control. He took his mother's hand and gave it a robust squeeze as the whole family looked on, agog.

The doctor set down his black leather bag, clicked it open then rummaged inside impatiently trying to free his tangled-up stethoscope and pull out anything else that might help. Surrounding the bed, all agonising, unable to decide what to do for the best, the Harvey family and the men looked to Doctor Croft for guidance (and a flicker of hope).

"Don't crowd the fellow," he ordered. "He needs clean, fresh air, not to be stifled and suffocated by you. Open the window, lad."

Richard ran to the window and opened it halfway to avoid a further ear-bashing from the doctor, hoping the room would not become too cold. The last thing his father needed was a chill. The four hewers trooped out obediently, not to be seen again, their work there done.

A tearful Hannah was inconsolable, shaking uncontrollably at the shock of seeing her husband. However, estranged they may have become over the years; he was still the father of their children.

"Take the good lady next door," counselled Dr Croft, finding her behaviour highly distracting.

Nell guided her mother to the study and sat her down.

"Come now, Mama, you need to gather your strength. Papa will need you as he recovers. We will need you."

A beleaguered Harriet had followed behind the two of them, finding the whole business extremely distressing, leaving Bess and Richard to help the doctor.

"Get some warm water, carbolic soap and some clean rags, Bess. We'll need to deal with those wounds to better assess his injuries and stop them worsening."

A few minutes later, returning to the bedroom with the requested items, she sat with the doctor, tending to her dear father's injuries. She sat on the empty side of the bed, where her stepmother normally slept, then curled her legs under her to kneel closer to her father. Leaning over, she dabbed at the bloodstains on his head with a clean white handkerchief she had wetted with the water. Gently caring for the broken man lying in front of her, she wasn't sure her efforts were improving his condition much. *Clearing his eyes, nose and mouth from this thick caking of dust will at least make him more comfortable.*

The doctor monitored Robert's pulse with a finger at his wrist, and his breathing with the stethoscope pressed onto his bruised chest. Earlier, with a firm yank, Dr Croft had set his broken upper arm back in position, and a splint had been fixed to it as a temporary measure.

Finally, able to croak a few words, Robert Harvey indicated he still felt an excruciating pain in his abdomen. His eyes were rolling again, and he groaned frequently.

The doctor lifted the lower edge of his patient's shirt and undid the first few buttons. He rested his stiffened right hand on his patient's belly and did his best to establish what was the matter. Pressing down firmly on his fingers with his other hand, he could feel the unmistakable signs of internal bleeding around the liver and spleen.

"I fear you have injured your intestines. There is not much I can do for that now, except monitor you overnight. Give you some pain relief. You might be too weak to survive the journey to hospi—" his voice trailed off, realising he had said too much.

On hearing that revelation, Bess did her best to blink away some tears and focused on the dabbing.

Next door, Hannah could still be heard to sob, feeling helpless. The soft, barely audible voices of her children did their best to soothe her anguish.

Richard visited Bess every half hour to relay updates to the family still in the study, but there wasn't much good news to be imparted. Robert was alive. That was the best they could hope for—for now.

Around two o'clock in the morning, Mr Harvey seemed to stabilise, even managed a smile for Bess, grateful she was there to tend to him. Pleased with his outward appearance and the improvements in his vital signs, Doctor Croft chanced the opportunity to return to his surgery to collect some more medicine, laudanum in particular.

"I'll return at six am to administer his next dose. If anything is to change, come for me immediately. You keep an eye on him, Miss Bess—his breathing and pulse as I showed you. You're doing a good job. Rest will be vital for him. He needs to regain his strength."

The doctor closed the door behind him, and his head sank with a sense of gloomy foreboding. Mr Harvey's chances were fifty-fifty at best, yet he had hinted to the relatives there would be a period of recuperation. *What else could I do? I have to keep a brave face and be optimistic about the situation.* He felt like he had just stretched the truth to its breaking point. Left alone, the daughter and her father enjoyed a tender moment together talking; him the patient, and her the nursemaid. The last time they had spoken at length was the fraught argument about the fiasco that was Mr Mortimer's spurned proposal. *Now, Bess regretted that deeply.*

Despite the awful circumstances, Bess was grateful for the chance to atone for her behaviour at least. *Perhaps I could learn to love Mr Mortimer. Once the shock of being engaged to him wears off. If he would still have me?*

Her father strained to touch her thoughtful face lightly on the cheek and said:

"I see you as my real daughter, Bess. Just as worthy of a father's love as the children Mrs Harvey blessed me with. I know life has been difficult because your stepmother has never accepted you. But my dear, I have. I have endeavoured to bring you up properly, no matter what the obstacles at times. I have struggled to give you a chance. I have tried to find you a good husband with the means to look after you. It is my duty as a good Christian father not to turn my back on my own. I won't be here forever."

"Shush, Father dearest," she said, resting her fingers on his dry and cracked mouth.

"I'm sorry I disappointed you with Mr Mortimer, Father. I will speak to him and accept his proposal if he is still agreeable."

"I think that ship has sailed, young Bess", said Mr Harvey with a faint, compassionate smile, also tinged with sadness.

"We shall find you a dashing fellow more your own age. Who couldn't love someone as graceful, educated and charming as you?"

Looking exhausted, his eyes flickered downwards and closed. Bess cradled his face in her hand to let him know she was still there. His breathing was strong and regular; his pulse the same. She was relieved to see him improving with some rest.

The bedroom door handled rattled as it opened. Mrs Harvey had finally summoned the strength to gather her composure. A brief conversation with the doctor in the hallway as he left had galvanised her.

"I'll sit with him now," she ordered, roughly pushing at Bess's shoulder to get her to move, then insisted she leave the room with a glare.

Bess's back had been aching from leaning over so long washing away the blood and dust, and the brief walk next door to see her brother and sisters helped ease the pain. Her heart, of course, was still torn in two with dread. *What if he doesn't pull through?* The children had gathered around a portrait of their father. It wasn't the same as a real bedside vigil, but their mother had forbidden them to go in the room, wanting to talk in private to her husband, in case it was her last chance to be with him alone.

The face in the painting had a strength about it, a strength they hoped their stricken father would be able to draw upon as he convalesced.

Every so often, one of them crept into the bedroom to ask Mrs Harvey if there had been any developments. There weren't. *'At least he wasn't getting any worse'*, they told themselves.

At half-past four in the morning, a piercing shriek came from the bedroom; a wrenching howl they had all been secretly expecting and dreading all the same.

Mr Robert Harvey was no more.

One by one, the children filed into the room to look at him, so horribly injured but at least peaceful. The frown lines on his face had smoothed out now, a little less in-grained than they had been these past few years. The weight of the world was no longer on his shoulders. It had now transferred to the rest of the Harvey household.

First thing in the morning, the funeral director, Albert Crump, was summoned. Robert's body was respectfully carried out of the family home feet first so he wouldn't look back into the house and beckon to someone else to join him on the other side.

13

MRS HARVEY'S
HELPFUL SUGGESTION

With the funeral behind them, Hannah and Richard turned their attention to business. Time was running out; the household coffers were in a perilous state. They had a difficult decision to make, to sell the hall or to sell the colliery, or both.

David Harvey had stepped in as an interim manager, but the elephant in the room still needed to be discussed. If Hannah hired new skilled managers to run the colliery, paying their wages meant she could no longer afford the upkeep for Walton Hall. With her hands tied, she intended to approach David to help her complete the sale and get a reasonable price for the pit.

Even with help, it would take time to find a buyer for the mine. Robert's brother was not interested in taking it on full-time. As the eldest of Robert's siblings, he was close to retirement age and was looking to scale down his workload, not increase it.

Selling the hall meant new homes would need to be found for the children. That was less of a problem. Harriet and Nell were already engaged. A partner for Richard would be relatively easy to find, he was a handsome young fellow, and if the engagement were secured before the news about selling the mine became common knowledge, he could probably find himself a decent bride.

Mrs Harvey had no interest whatsoever in helping Bess. The thought of her being in the workhouse was appealing, but she knew that would drive a wedge between her and her own children; they had, unfathomably, warmed to the urchin.

Hannah decided to discuss her options for Bess with her eldest daughter. Over afternoon tea, they hatched a plan.

"The match your father planned between her and Mr Mortimer has gone sour. The ignorant girl spurned his offer."

"He was almost three times her age and widowed twice already, Mother," added Harriet in Bess's defence.

"So, we will find somebody who is more her age, and is as yet unmarried then she cannot object to him. I will be free of her at last. I know just the fellow."

"But who?" enquired the daughter.

"Never mind. Leave it to me," said a determined Hannah Harvey.

She dismissed Harriet with a waft of her hand towards the door and a stern look to reinforce the point. Then she called Meg in.

She began penning a note for her servant to take into Woodborough when she did her errands later that day. Meg looked on as the lady of the house furiously scribbled the message down, without a single correction needed.

"Use your discretion. Make sure no-one is in the shop when you pass this message on and make sure it is read in front of you."

"Yes, Ma'am" confirmed Meg, curious why Mrs Harvey would send a secret handwritten order to a shopkeeper.

Maybe it's not an order? Perhaps money is so tight she needs to pay in instalments. I wonder who it's destined for?

"May I ask the nature of the note, Ma'am?"

Losing patience, Mrs Harvey added:

"No, you may not. It's none of your business—Don't just stand there. Take this and get back to work."

Meg scurried off to collect her wicker shopping basket and promptly made her way to the High Street, with Mrs Harvey looking out of the dining room window to make sure her envoy had left.

The handwritten note was addressed to the owner of the hardware store. John Giddings was a single, well-built, polite man, about ten years older than Bess and rumoured to require a wife. His dowager aunt had recently died, leaving no one to care for him and his elderly father. With two rooms above the shop and a large sitting room with a range, there was plenty of space for a wife to move in and set up a home.

Her errands meant visiting several shops. Picking an unusual, inefficient route, she had plenty of opportunities to walk past the hardware store to check it was empty. On the third pass, seeing Mr Giddings alone, she seized the moment.

"A note for you, Sir. From the lady of Walton Hall, Mrs 'arvey."

"Oh. How is she fairing? I heard the terrible news about her husband. Taken from us well before his time—" his voice petered out as he took a moment to reflect as a sign of respect.

"Yes, it has been quite a shock for us all."

Meg urged Mr Giddings to open the note there and then, with an enquiring rise of her eyebrows. Opening the envelope, he began to read.

"I'll leave you to read it. I'll wait here, in case you need to send a message back." said an intrigued Meg.

"Right you are," replied the distracted shopkeeper.

After a torturous wait, Meg was put out of her misery.

"I've been asked to afternoon tea at the house on Sunday to discuss an important personal matter, but it does not say what."

Not being one to gossip, Meg left without telling a puzzled Mr Giddings why he had been summoned. *So, has she chosen him for Bess?*

Sunday could not come soon enough for the hardware shop owner. As instructed, he arrived at the porch of Walton Hall at four o'clock sharp, checked he looked presentable, then rang the doorbell.

He was greeted by Meg and ushered to the parlour, where an austere-looking Mrs Harvey waited alone, clad in a black crinoline dress, with the mirrors covered and the clock stopped at 4.30 as a mark of respect for her late husband.

"Thank you for coming, Mr Giddings. I do appreciate you being amenable to my request. Please, take a seat. Would you like a slice of sponge cake, freshly made this afternoon?"

"That sounds splendid, Mrs Harvey. Thank you."

She was positively oozing with uncharacteristic pleasantness. Meg began to serve the refreshments.

"May I enquire as to why you have asked me here today, Mrs Harvey. Do you need to order hardware supplies for the pit?"

"Oh, it's not goods that I want. Mr Giddings. It's not goods at all."

The shopkeeper looked confused. The lady of the house paused, waiting for Meg to leave.

"Do you want to know what I need? Quite simply, I require you to propose to the orphan niece that my husband and I took in many years ago, Bess. You must have seen her at church and around Woodborough?"

A speechless John Giddings nodded, taking a big bite of cake as he listened. His chewing meant he could play for a few valuable seconds to think as he came to terms with Mrs Harvey's idea.

"I understand you and your father live alone these days, without a lady of the house to care for you? She's at a marriageable age and an educated young lady. I'm sure she will be a most excellent wife for you."

He was stunned at Mrs Harvey's forthright request. However, he'd had his head turned by Bess when she strolled through the market square with her siblings, and her beauty was widely spoken of by the young men in the area.

> "She has gone for a walk whilst we discussed her situation, Mr Giddings. But on her return, this will be your opportunity to make your proposal. Another cup of tea whilst you wait?"

> "She hardly knows me, Mrs Harvey" he replied, feeling very dull in comparison to the striking beauty of Bess.

> "I have explained the situation to her. With Robert—my husband—now dearly departed, she knows it is time for her to find a spouse and not dally any longer. She is one of the last of my children to be engaged, and will do what is expected of her."

After a further hour of excruciatingly polite conversation, it was clear Bess's walk was taking longer than anticipated.

Eager to get out of a household clearly in mourning, the shopkeeper offered to go, suggesting to a grateful Mrs Harvey that she send Bess to see him in the week when he would most definitely propose.

With that, he got up to leave. Sarah escorted him to the front door, noticing he looked much happier than when he arrived.

Bess's sunny afternoon stroll that day was again a wonderful breath of fresh air. The atmosphere in the house had been tense after the death of her father, especially for Bess, who wasn't sure how she was supposed to react—as distraught as the closest family members—or less so. It was all very unsettling.

The strict rules of mourning had brought a sombre tone to the house. All the children felt the burden of the impending sale of the colliery and probably the hall. The sense of upheaval was unbearable. Under the circumstances, a walk would always seem preferable.

She took her usual route down along the lane between the hall and the Hamilton estate towards Woodborough, and quickly became lost in thought, focusing what the loss of her father would mean. Apart from making sure she didn't fall in one of the potholes again, she paid scant attention to her surroundings that day. She didn't notice Harry walking up the lane towards her until they were barely six feet apart.

There was a brief awkward silence until he managed to say:

"Sorry to hear about your father, Bess. It must have been an awful shock."

She bit her lip briefly to compose herself, then replied:

"Yes, it has been hard. Mrs Harvey has taken it particularly badly. I've had to come out of the house. The atmosphere is unbearable." She sighed. "Mrs Harvey is keen for us all to find partners. Now that our—"

Bess thought it inappropriate to air their dirty laundry in public but also rude to end speaking abruptly, mid-sentence, so she carried on. *Harry could be trusted, surely?*

"Our domestic circumstances have changed. Of course, she isn't able to run the mine herself and covering the cost of hiring someone with experience to manage it for us is prohibitively expensive. With all the children soon to be married, she plans to move nearer her family, the Carlyles, in Lancashire. Get a much smaller cottage, alone and live off the proceeds. My father thought it best for Mr Mortimer to ask me to marry him to provide for me—" She trailed off. Harry understood Bess's reticence to marry a widowed man more than twice her age.

"It's going to be difficult for you Bess without your father's protection, that's for sure. Mr Harvey did an exemplary job of caring for you after your mother passed and all."

"I know. My stepmother plans for me to find a husband—I know she does."

"Well, your status is higher now, Bess. Choose well. You can make a real mark on the world, thanks to that schooling of yours."

Bess looked to his kind face and wished it could be Harry that she was to marry. *Why did he have to be taken? How can a man who lives so alone in a far corner of that estate ever meet a woman and fall in love? Why didn't he choose me? He must have known I would come back once board-ing school was over?*

Harry was a straightforward soul, one of the few people that she could genuinely relate to. He was someone who understood the kind person that she was. She wasn't the orphan. She wasn't the stepsister. She wasn't the para-site. She was Bess.

"Would you care to walk with me into Woodborough, Harry?" she asked.

"I can't, Miss. I've got urgent work to do on the estate for Lord Hamilton. He's organising a shooting party in the next few days with his aristocratic chums."

"Right you are," she said, looking at him as he started to turn away, the words "Bye then, Miss," drifting after him.

Bess continued her walk. She was wracking her brains to think of who her stepmother might match her with. *Mr Mortimer had ruled himself out (hopefully), but who else could Mrs Harvey choose?*

She wished she had the money to run away start and again, be an unknown woman with a few bobs' worth of savings behind her, but that wasn't an option. She had no nest egg at all, and she anticipated none of the meagre inheritance from selling the family's assets would pass to her, especially as there was the mortgage and some busi-ness debts still outstanding. The support she had received to date would be her one 'windfall' in life.

She walked through Woodborough but found it anything but relaxing. Everyone knew her father had recently died and wanted to pay their respects. She was touched but also found it draining. Just for that afternoon, Bess wished to break from the misery and grief. She treated herself to a cup of hot chocolate at the tea shop near the railway station with the last few pence she had in her pocket. She stirred in some sugar, then sipped at the warm, sweet liquid and felt instantly comforted by it. A few minutes later, she was thanking the busy maid, who told her for a second time she was sad to hear the news of her late father and then made her way back to Walton Hall.

The next few days dragged. The family home was quiet and was soon to get quieter still. Harriet was due to move out once she married William Burridge. She was often sat alone, packing and repacking the belongings she planned to take with her. Nell was preparing herself to live with some of Mrs Harvey's relatives while she was in training. It made her closer to her future husband. Richard was away most of the time, organising the sale of the mine with Uncle David, and showing prospective buyers around. He still had no fiancée.

Most of the time, when Bess was in the house, she sat in her room alone, desperate to avoid Mrs Harvey for fear of upsetting her and getting into trouble again. Other times, she sat down at the boathouse, wishing Harry would walk by.

14

THE BOLT OUT OF THE BLUE

The next day Bess decided to take another walk into Woodborough, partly in case she bumped into Harry and partly because once again the freedom of the countryside was better than the stifling atmosphere in the house.

With a wicker basket on her arm to suggest she had a purpose for her stroll, she made her way down towards the High Street, politely greeting the shopkeepers as they tended to their goods on the pavement. She passed the cobbler, the baker, and the butcher. Each one brought up the subject of her late father, and her progress was slow. The weather was turning stormy, and a stiff breeze was making her black shawl and bonnet frill flap violently. The harsh weather matched the turmoil she felt inside. She walked like she was in a trance, placing one foot in front of the other, staring down at the pavement to keep her face out of the wind and avoid eye contact with yet more well-wishers with condolences. When she came to, she found herself in front of the hardware store. Battling against the gale, one side of her dress was glued onto her skin, the other side flapping like triangles of bunting at a fête.

The shopfront was well presented. There as a door on the right, and above that and the display window was a neatly painted black sign with gold lettering, Giddings Hardware Emporium. On the wall hung some galvanised pails. A few wicker baskets outside the shop displayed some of the cheaper items. Inside, all sorts of the latest inventions and curios were neatly stacked in the shop window, tins of specialist French polishes and bottles of cleaning solutions promising miracles. The new-fangled safety matches caught her eye too.

Seeing her pause outside the shop, Mr Giddings took it upon himself to scurry out from behind his counter and met her by the entrance.

"Why don't you come in, Miss, warm yourself with a hot drink—get out of this bad weather? I expect everyone's asking you about your father and you could do with a rest from that? It's nice and private out at the back. What do you say? Our kettle is always on the boil. A cup of tea, perhaps?"

"That would be lovely, Mr Giddings," said a thankful Bess, stepping inside the shop.

"Come on through," he said, beckoning her with his right arm, sweeping it towards the back of his shop and the small doorway that led to the Giddings' spacious sitting room.

Bess sensed George Giddings curiously looking at his son, and she couldn't decide why. She put it down to him feeling irritated John had decided to down tools to be sympathetic to her needs, leaving him on his own to deal with customers.

"Take a seat, Miss."

Bess was offered the comfy-looking rocking chair to the left of the fireplace. It was plush and velvety, and she settled into it, grateful for the kindness that was being shown to her. Being in the spotlight with the constant expectation to mourn her dead father publicly was challenging.

John Giddings took the kettle off the range and made two strong teas in some very delicate China cups, quite out of proportion for such a heavy-boned man. He passed one to Bess which she gratefully accepted.

"I wanted to say something to you—" he said, then paused, seeming thoughtful and tongue-tied.

In an attempt to alleviate his awkwardness, Bess added sympathetically:

"Do continue—" and gave him an encouraging smile.

"Miss Harvey, how do I put this—" He stopped again, fighting for the right words. Although he had earnestly practised what he planned to say for hours now, when the moment came, words failed him.

"The thing is, Miss—"

"Yes?"

"After a discussion with Mrs Harvey, can I ask, would you do me the honour of becoming my wife?"

On hearing this revelatory news, Bess's chair stopped rocking, and she looked intently at the kind man in front of her.

"You look surprised, Miss—" said the crestfallen shopkeeper.

She was.

"Mrs Harvey gave me the impression that you would be aware of my imminent proposal. She invited me up to Walton Hall—to talk to me about it. I thought she would have spoken to you too? It looks like my actions have come as something of a shock."

"I don't know what to say, Mr Giddings. I am flattered that you think I should become your wife. Of course, I will need time to consider. Please don't think me rude or dismissive. It's just the—surprise of it all. What with my father's passing this month too. I am quite taken aback. You do understand."

He sensed that Bess looked a little hurt. He decided that she was disappointed her stepmother had thought a lowly shopkeeper to be a suitable match for her. He knew nothing about her feelings for Harry Sutherland. No one did.

"I will give you my decision tomorrow, Mr Giddings, I promise. Now, please excuse me, I must speak to my family."

She smiled earnestly, hoping he would realise she would say yes once she was used to the idea. Reluctantly, he nodded. Bess was pleased he seemed far less pushy than Mr Mortimer, and he respected her need for a little space to think.

She put down her cup and walked through the shop, under the watchful gaze of a disappointed George Giddings, who had been busying himself snooping in on the entire conversation by the doorway. Battling the wind, Bess hurried back to Walton Hall.

During her absence, Richard Harvey had spoken to his mother and was keen to hear his sister would be engaged.

"Have you got some important news from Woodborough, Bess?" he enquired.

"If you mean am, I betrothed to Mr Giddings", she said through gritted teeth, "well—I didn't tell him no. In fact, I didn't answer either way."

In a split second, Richard's expression gave her a look that meant her behaviour was utterly unacceptable. To appease him and to explain her conduct she advised:

"Tomorrow, I will see him and say yes. I needed the night to sleep on it. I was being coy."

Richard looked at her, amazed that she thought it satisfactory to spurn a second carefully arranged proposal. *Did she not understand the changing family fortunes? Time was running out. Honestly. Mr Giddings is a hard-working, conscientious man with a shop and a home. She could fare a lot worse. She can't afford to be picky unless she wants to face the workhouse?*

15

THE ACCEPTANCE

A fuming stepmother stormed into Bess's room a few minutes after she slid off from speaking to her brother hoping to hide away from another inquisition.

"How dare you disobey me, girl? Richard told me you have delayed your response to Mr Giddings proposal. What are you playing at? A woman like you ought to be glad anyone would take you on. Without my husband taking pity on you, goodness knows how low you would have sunk? The other children seem to be able to follow instructions. You will leave this household, and you will marry Mr Giddings."

"As soon as possible," she added, leaving Bess to her thoughts.

There was no point trying to improve her lot. Besides, what was there to improve? Life at the shop—with him— would be bearable, perhaps even agreeable with time.

And, there were no better offers on the table, nor likely to be.

She walked down towards the boating shed, then broke into a run. The weather had brightened a little even if Bess's mood had not. Seeing her emotional flee from the hall, Meg put the laundry down and followed behind, struggling to keep up with the pace.

She hoped there was something she could do to help the girl, even it was just a shoulder to cry on. It was heart-breaking to see her so sad. Fifty yards or more behind, she followed Bess down towards the lake. But instead of stopping, Bess carried on, down the path towards the gamekeeper's cottage.

Meg began to see why Bess was so emotional, putting two and two together, or rather one and one and working out the answer to the question. She knew the girl had a soft spot for the handsome, kind and protective Harry ever since he had found her years earlier, perhaps even saving her life that night? *That must have made an impression on her?* Meg was surprised that such a good man was still unmarried. *It must be because of the odd hours he works, and being stuck out there on his own. Perhaps Bess was about to break tradition and ask him to marry her? Bess always did have a rebellious streak. She must have got that from her unabashed mother? She wasn't afraid to go after what she wanted.*

Bess saw Harry's sheepdog tethered to a metal post, ly-ing on a few smooth, grey flagstones, just to the left-hand corner of the cottage. Sometimes, she'd confide in Jasper, on finding him alone. He was a good listener and didn't judge her harshly and order her about like other people seem to of late. *He can be trusted to keep a secret.* Their private conversations always seemed to give her a fresh perspective on her woes, even though all Jasper could really do was look at her. She wondered what advice he might have for her today to solve another ghastly predicament.

She slid down against the post, keeping her dress out of the mud by tucking it onto the flagstones, then put her arm softly around the dog's neck and began to unburden her soul. Jasper listened placidly, breathing quietly, his ears twitching inquisitively.

After a few minutes, she ran out of things to say, too sad to put her thoughts into words. She decided to take comfort simply stroking Jasper's glossy black and white fur.

Back in the direction of the hall, Meg hid behind some bushes as close as she could, fearing the dog would bark and break her cover. *In the next life, Jasper, I will be with my Harry, I will.* Some footsteps sounded on the gravel, Harry's footsteps. Jasper had noticed them, but a troubled Bess had not. The first thing she knew of it was when the dog stood and wagged his tail to greet his master.

"You alright, Miss?" said Harry, seeing her watery eyes, red and puffy with pent up frustration.

"Please don't be kind to me."

You've already decided you don't want to be a mistress. It's time to say goodbye, Bess. But she couldn't quite manage to utter the words though. Not yet, at least.

"No. No, I'm fine, Harry. Please, carry on as you were. You've got work to do. I have some errands needing attention. I only came to check Jasper had some water," she lied.

Harry made a move towards her and tried to take her hand. She collected her skirts and fled back towards Walton Hall, feeling it was less of a home and more of a prison these days, able to squash her dreams like a fly swat brutally and decisively smears its prey against a wall.

Meg waited a few minutes for the going to be clear, then sneaked back to her chores.

At the door, Bess decided it was too soon to go back, and she opted to take the other lane towards the outskirts of Woodborough and the railway station. The route would keep her well away from the Giddings Hardware Emporium. She didn't want Mrs Harvey revelling in seeing her so distraught. It would add to the misery of her situation.

She'd almost reached town when who should she bump into but her sister, Nell. She had taken the train to Foxton earlier that day to see the other branch of the Carlyle clan, headed by Hannah's younger brother to discuss when she would move in. Deciding a stop at the tea shop for a catch up would be in order, they delayed their return to Walton Hall.

An excitable Nell jabbered away about her latest news. Bess was pleased to see one of them, at least, seemed genuinely happy with their future.

"I can't wait to become a pupil-teacher, Bess. I know it is a difficult job, but being able to stay with the Carlyles is a way out of Walton. It's just not the same without Papa. The wages are not great, and I'll have to pass on most of it as board and lodgings, but at least it gets me away from mother—and it gives me time to get to know Jonathan before we are married. We spent some time together today. He is so thoughtful. He gave me this. I feel so guilty for thinking him boring at the party!"

Nell pointed to an exquisite, delicate necklace then looked at Bess's face for her reaction. There wasn't one, her gaze was distant, and her eyes unfocused. Suddenly feeling awkward about talking about herself so much, Nell changed the subject.

"There I go, harping on about myself again. I'm sorry. You look troubled Bess. I can be so selfish at times."

She took her sister's trembling hand.

"What's wrong? Tell me," she asked solemnly.

"Mrs Harvey has found me a suitor."

"She has?" said an intrigued Nell.

"Yes. And of course, I have to accept—" Bess paused slightly as she spoke for fear of crying again. "It's Mr Giddings, the hardware shopkeeper. I walked past the shop recently and he invited me in, and because of the terrible weather at the time, I accepted. We took some tea at the back of his shop, in his sitting room, and before I knew it, he'd proposed, right out of the blue. I have barely said a word to him since I came to Woodborough. I have never had any need for the merchandise in his shop. I played for time saying that I would give him my answer later when we had spoken as a family. He knew I was lying since he was well aware it was your Mama who had hatched the scheme—without telling me anything."

"But what's there to think about, Bess? He seems a good fellow? He's cheerful enough. He's dependable, and he has his own business. Plus, he's not been married before—or twice before—unlike that old curmudgeon, Mr Mortimer. You will be free of Mama. I know how hard it is that she's never accepted you, Bess. It's time to move on. You'll soon get used to your new life. Besides, none of us can stay at the hall any longer. It's just weeks away from sale. The die is cast."

"I know, Nell. Beggars can't be choosers. But I fear my heart belongs to another and if I can't marry him, part of me doesn't want anybody. I know that's only a daydream, but just for one more day, I wanted to imagine I could have married my prince—"

"Who is it, Bess? Who's captured your heart?"

"It doesn't matter, Nell. He's married. I found out recently, after years of secretly being in love with him, hoping he would notice me. But of course, I am far too plain—and too late," she lamented.

"I will become Mrs Giddings," she concluded with a heavy heart.

Many a young girl loved calling themselves by their husband's surname to see how it felt. Some lucky betrothed couples, carved their soon-to-be-married initials in the bark of a tree, smitten with affection. Bess was heartbroken at the mere thought of being forced to become a Giddings and everything that new name would inevitably entail.

"Come on, let's go back, it's getting late," said Nell.

As the two girls walked up the driveway to Walton Hall, Meg opened the door for them. They found Mrs Harvey in the parlour with the door to the hallway wide open, waiting for them.

"Ah, do tell me your news, Nell" she demanded, keen to prove that at least one of her daughters could follow her instructions accurately. "Join me for some tea."

The two girls immediately followed the order. Hannah retook her favourite seat close to the window.

"Nell, do tell me how you got on at my brother's house today."

"Yes, Mama. My visit was enjoyable. The Carlyles are happy for me to live there. Their eldest daughter has recently married, and I can lodge in her old room. My board will cost most of my wages, but there will be a shilling or two leftover in the month for some treats. When I am married to Jonathan, we will have a good life. Until I have a child, I will continue to work."

"That's wonderful news. It's good to see you flourishing," said Mrs Harvey cheerfully, mainly to make Bess feel guilty, who unlike Nell, always seemed to delight in defying her.

"We have some good news too, don't we Bess?" she continued, eager to reinforce that her illegitimate daughter had finally reached the end of the line with her marital prevarication.

Bess nodded in agreement and defeat.

"Yes, young Bess here is going to marry Mr Giddings down in Woodborough, the hardware store owner, I'm sure you know him, Nell. He is a good, honest fellow who will provide for her."

"I am sure he will, Mama," added Nell, reinforcing to Bess what her course of action should be.

"For some reason, she decided to be coy about the matter, but Bess is going to accept his proposal tomorrow—aren't you?" said Mrs Harvey authoritatively.

Bess nodded, trying not to frown at the same time.

"Now, I have work to do for the sale of the colliery. Richard is due to meet me at any minute to discuss an offer from one of the potential buyers. Why don't you girls go off and get ready for dinner? For once, we all have something to celebrate in this household."

That night Bess found sleep eluded her. She did her best to look for the good in her situation but found little to cheer about. *The sooner I say yes, the sooner I will be out of purgatory and my new life can begin, and the sooner I can start to shape my future.*

That morning, she walked to the hardware shop with purpose and told Mr Giddings that she would gladly accept his kind proposal.

He ran to Bess and squeezed her so tightly in his arms he felt she would break in two. He was delighted that he would have a good woman to look after him; and being a kind soul, he was looking forward to taking care of her too. With his father still living with him, he had never really been able to assert his position as the head of the household. Once he had a wife, his status would be enhanced, and he would, at last, be master in his own home.

Bess walked feeling lost and alone, knowing that the next conversation she would have to have would be planning the date for the wedding with her stepmother; assuming that too hadn't been set already with Howard Swinnerton, the vicar, in her absence.

16

THE WEDDING

After some preparations, the morning of Bess's wedding day finally arrived. Mr Giddings was eager for the ceremony to start. He stood at the altar, waiting for his lovely bride to appear, his father was by his side. They were both wearing their best clothes. The groom looked straight ahead, bursting with pride, smiling at Reverend Swinnerton, the man who would make his dream (at least) come true. The church was full of the great and the good folk of Woodborough. Doctor Croft, Mr Mortimer, as well as some members of Mr Harvey's family, his brother David and his household in particular. Only the closest members of the Burridge and Carlyle family were present.

The hubbub of voices in the background promptly faded, and a silence fell amongst the congregation. Hearing the peal of church bells to signal her arrival, John Giddings turned around and smiled at his gorgeous bride to be, keen to start the next phase of his life—to protect and nurture her and start a family of his own.

The organist took his seat and played the fashionable accompaniment to the walk up the aisle to—Felix Mendelssohn's 'Wedding March'.

David Harvey, who had agreed to give his niece away, slowly paced alongside Bess, a vision of loveliness, in a simple but beautiful white dress, her unruly hair perfectly styled. Pretty petals had been scattered in the aisle to bring the couple good luck. Behind them, walked the bridesmaids, Harriet and Nell.

Bess moved with poise, grace and charm, shyly smiling as she walked. Inside she was devoid of any sense of love or excitement. She felt more like a condemned prisoner being led to the gallows, not a young woman giving herself freely to the love of her life.

This wasn't the life she had expected, nor wanted, but compared with the workhouse or years of spinsterhood with a life of servitude like Meg or Sarah, it was the more palatable option.

Bess gave John a nervous, but alluring smile, thinking that if she was going to have to make herself love him, today was the day to start. At least he wasn't cruel and spiteful like Frederick Carlyle, or old enough to be her father, like Edward Mortimer. The groom clearly idolised her. *Things will work out for us. They'll have to.*

David Harvey left her by the side of her intended and took his seat in the front row next to sister-in-law, Hannah, prominently dressed in her mourning clothes, with the two bridesmaids taking their places at the end of the second pew.

Smiling at the young couple in front of him, the vicar greeted the throng and began the ceremony.

"Dearly beloved, we are gathered together here in the sight of God, and in the face of this congregation, to join together this man and this woman in holy matrimony; which is an honourable estate, instituted of God in the time of man's innocence, signifying unto us the mystical union that is betwixt Christ and his church."

John Giddings turned a little to gauge Bess's mood. She was looking ahead, motionless, more like a waxwork, than a person.

The vicar continued.

"Therefore it is not, by any, to be enterprised, nor taken in hand, unadvisedly, lightly, or wantonly, to satisfy men's carnal lusts and appetites, like brute beasts that have no understanding; but reverently, discreetly, advisedly, soberly, and in the fear of God; duly considering the causes for which matrimony was ordained."

The door at the back creaked open, and there was the clatter of a few footsteps as the latecomer took their place in the last of the pews on the left-hand side of the church. Bess wondered who the straggler was, but was unable to see. Had she been able to look, she would see Harry Sutherland had crept in, uninvited.

The service continued.

"I require and charge you both, as you will answer at the dreadful day of judgement when the secrets of all hearts shall be disclosed, that if either of you or any persons here present know any impediment, why you may not be lawfully joined together in matrimony, you do now confess it."

Howard Swinnerton paused for what seemed like an eternity for the anxious groom then continued with the service.

Turning to a relieved John Giddings, the vicar asked:

"Wilt thou have this woman, Elizabeth Mary Harvey, to be thy lawful wedded wife, to live together after God's ordinance in the holy estate of matrimony? Wilt thou love her, comfort her, honour, and keep her in sickness and in health; and, forsaking all other, keep thee only unto her, so long as you both shall live?"

"I will," came the solemn reply.

The vicar turned to Bess and invited her to look towards her betrothed. Out of the corner of her eye, she could now see the dark, brooding figure of Harry Sutherland at the back. The pain in her heart was excruciating. She barely managed to focus. A dizzying blur of thoughts raced through her mind.

"Wilt thou have this man, John William Giddings to be thy lawful wedded husband, to live together after God's ordinance in the holy estate of matrimony? Wilt thou obey him, and serve him, love, honour, and keep him in sickness and in health; and, forsaking all other, keep thee only unto him, so long as you both shall live?"

Having inhaled deeply during the vicar's delivery, Bess let the breathy words tumble out of her lungs, almost forcing her body to say, "I will."

She fell into a trance as John said his vows, holding her hand tenderly, gazing at her fondly, but she was not under the spell of love, more resignation to her fate. An absent-minded, self-defence mechanism had taken over her. The vicar sensing her anxiety spoke her words to be repeated just a few at a time, in case she struggled to remember. She was clearly under quite some strain.

John proudly guided a glittering gold ring onto Bess's finger, whence they kneeled down.

"Let us pray. O eternal God, creator and preserver of all mankind, giver of all spiritual grace, the author of everlasting life; send thy blessing upon these thy servants, this man and this woman, whom we bless in thy name. Just as Isaac and Rebecca lived faithfully together, so these persons may surely perform and keep the vow and covenant betwixt them made, (whereof this ring given and received is a token and pledge,) and may ever remain in perfect love and peace together, and live according to thy laws; through Jesus Christ our Lord. Amen."

He joined the newlyweds' right hands together, then said:

"Those whom God hath joined together let no man put asunder."

Full of joy and love, John Giddings looked earnestly into Bess's eyes and kissed her for the first time, briefly and delicately, before the onlooking congregation.

After the parish register was signed in the vestry, the couple returned to the altar. Mrs Harvey, still in her mourning dress, broke with tradition and led the wedding party out, accompanied by David. Believing the folklore, she hoped her prominence as a widow at the service would bring bad luck on Bess, even if Mr Giddings might be innocently caught in the crossfire. Mrs Harvey was soon to move away and could not have cared less what happened to her late husband's accursed progeny.

Walking proudly down the aisle and outside into a cool, crisp morning, John Giddings could not have been happier. Bess took some comfort that at least now the deed was done, and the more comfortable period of adjustment could begin.

Hannah and Nell pinned wedding favours on the shoulders of the guests outside the church, then some small handfuls of nuts were thrown over the couple to bless the fertility of their union. The groom pulled his bride gently towards him and swept her up in his strong arms, kissing her tenderly for the second time. Bess felt herself giving in to her new circumstances, despite sensing the piercing eyes of Harry Sutherland on her.

The kiss was cut short when a young lad, Joseph Burton, came running up the path towards the church, his wooden clogs knocking loudly on the cobbles.

"Come quickly! Come quickly! There's a fire down on the High Street, flames puthering out of the bakers and it's spreading fast."

Many of the wedding guests were Mr Giddings' shop-keeping neighbours, and quickly a herd of panicked men were running towards their premises. John kissed Bess softly and whispered, "Stay here and be safe, my love. I will be back for you soon," then pulled away.

"You stay here and look after my wife", he said to George, knowing his ageing father would not be able to run to the scene and didn't want to embarrass him about his frailty.

Bess accompanied George Giddings to the bench by the church lichgate. The shock of the rapid turn of events had made him unsteady on his feet. She sat with him and tried to calm his anxiety about potentially losing their livelihood. After a couple of minutes, Bess offered to walk towards the start of the High Street to find out what was going on and promised to return immediately.

Seeing his chance, Harry Sutherland shouted he would help save the shops too, giving him a reason to run towards her—even though she was Mrs Giddings and now unavailable. Thinking the old man's sight wouldn't be great, when he guessed he was far enough away, he desperately grabbed Bess's upper arms and turned her to face him. There was a hint of alcohol on his breath.

"I wish I'd dared to ask you to marry me, Bess. It near broke my heart to see you wedded to another man today," he confessed. "I always thought the Harveys would have you betrothed to one of those well-to-do Carlyles or Burridges like your sisters, not a humble gamekeeper like me."

"Stop being horrid. Playing tricks on me. You've just watched me get hitched. And I know you have chosen another woman, Harry Sutherland, I saw her at your cottage. She was doing the laundry, pegging out your undergarments—only wives do that. She had a wedding ring on. I know you're married, Harry. Stop lying. Stay away from me."

Harry looked on as her wild eyes flashed angrily at him.

"You don't understand, Bess. She's one of the servants from the estate who's took pity on me and does chores around the cottage. It's a benefit of the gamekeeper's position. Means the Lord can get away with paying me less. She's no wife of mine."

Bess almost collapsed at the news, speechless. Her knees buckled in shock. *But that means I've married the wrong man. Nothing was stopping me following my heart with Father dead.* Harry grabbed her to steady her, just like he had when she stumbled into the pothole in the lane to Walton Hall.

She had loved the sense of his strong touch, but it felt different now she was married. His advances were now inappropriate. Confused, angry and lost, she pushed him away, making her disappointment in the situation clear.

"You're too late, Harry. I'm another man's wife now and that's the end of it."

Thwarted, and not wishing to risk drawing attention to their tryst any longer, Harry Sutherland ran off towards the fire to offer his assistance.

Back at the bench, wearing his gold-rimmed glasses to get a better view of the shops, a seething George Giddings had also seen the tender moment between the two doomed lovers. Every muscle in his frail old body clenched like iron. *How dare she carry on like that? With another fellow in broad daylight? On her wedding day? My poor son. What has he gotten himself into?*

17

MR STRICKLAND'S HEADACHE

The bright morning weather was now replaced by dark menacing storm clouds and thick smoke filling the air. The rain began to hammer down, and there was a chill in the air.

Seeing George Giddings now sheltering alone under the lichgate, the vicar offered to take him to the nearby pub to get him warm.

"The Lord is helping us by sending us this rain, George. I am sure the fire will be under control very soon. Try not to worry too much."

George Giddings, however, was very worried. He shuffled over the uneven cobbles towards the Railway Arms, with a nervous vicar by his side, fearing he could have a bad fall at any moment.

Bess slowly made her way towards the smoke billowing up from the High Street. Even if she wasn't going to be able to fight the fire herself, at least she could offer moral support. She felt it proper to see if the spreading fire had spared the hardware store—or not. Although she didn't have a romantic interest in her husband yet, at least she did care about his—their—welfare.

She approached the cobbler's shop and saw Harry's strong arms collecting bucketsful of water from the pond, and passing them to the next man in the line, him onto the next man and so on until the water could douse the flames. For a split second, they gazed at each other. He looked heartbroken. The connection between them was palpable, and yet their union could never be.

The rain was getting worse, but it was helping to contain the spread of the fire. The few minutes it had been going had caused devastation for the baker's shop. The flames billowed from the windows, fluttering menacingly like deadly orangey-yellow ribbons. The heat was incredible, sharply tingling Bess's face from quite a distance away. Out of the roof, the fire's red-hot embers shot up and drifted gracefully downwards threatening to set everything alight in their path. The roofs that were thatched looked ready to set ablaze at any moment. There was a good chance the inferno would make its way along inside the roof spaces and destroy the neighbouring premises. Only five doors away from the baker's, the hardware store was in grave danger.

Bess looked on, her short-sleeved wedding dress caked in mud around the ankles, and her wet hair was plastered against her head. The petals had been beaten away from the fresh flowers that had adorned her hair, the gigantic raindrops smashing into them like tiny cannon balls.

The thick, acrid smell of smouldering wood settling in the High Street, was making it difficult to breathe. It stung the eyes of those near it, forcing them to blink hard for a moment of relief.

The fire had begun to take hold of the roof next to the bakers with a fearful John Giddings looking at the two smouldering, blackened shops as they crackled and creaked.

Stood alone on the periphery of the fiery crisis, Bess felt let down and deceived, trapped in an hours-old loveless marriage. The situation could have been avoided if she and Harry had been far less coy and a lot more honest about their true feelings when she first came back to Woodborough. What's more, the thin veil of security that being a shopkeeper's wife was supposed to offer was now at risk of being destroyed by the fire. *Can this get any worse?*

Both John and Harry turned to see Bess choking in the haze. Harry yelled:

"You tend to your shop, Mr Giddings. I'll escort your young lady to the Railway Arms for shelter, then come to help you. She'll catch her death in this awful weather."

"Thank you, Sir. I'll be back there to look after you soon, my love, I promise," replied a panic-stricken John, doing his best to look like he was somehow in control.

As they walked the short distance the pub, Bess was all in a dither. Every fibre in her body was telling her to act with restraint and decorum, but it became too much. Her feet felt stuck to the ground, the gravity of her situation weighing heavily upon her.

"God strike me down, but I love you, Harry Sutherland. I always have. From the minute you cared for me when I was injured in the boathouse all those years ago. You are one of the few people to have shown me kindness and understanding, treating me like an equal, rather than an outsider. And now—"

Bess sobbed uncontrollably.

"Shush, shush," said Harry trying to soothe her angst. He couldn't bear to hear any more.

"I don't want to sound wicked, Harry, but I wish the shop roof would collapse around John and take him down with it, so we could be together."

"You mustn't talk that way, Bess. Be careful what you wish for."

Harry took her arm and led her the short distance to the pub, left her at the doorway, then hurried back to help with putting out the fire. They had no idea they had been spotted a second time that day by George Giddings. *Him again! Sniffing around another man's wife like he hasn't a care in the world! Has he no shame?*

George Giddings played dumb as Bess sat beside him. Biting his tongue about the treachery that had come to light, he vowed to speak to his son as soon as he came to collect them. *My boy has had enough suffering for one day, surely. I wish I could turn the clock back for him and spare him from these disasters. He doesn't know half of the predicament he's in. This selfish shrew could be the devil's own daughter with her lascivious behaviour today!*

Seeing the old man deep in thought, Bess anticipated it was the shop weighing on his mind and tried to comfort him.

> "The men are doing their best to douse the flames, Mr Giddings. It seems to be more under control out there. It's not touched the shop yet," she volunteered, not really knowing if that were still true or not.

Back at Woodborough's pond, the men were working hard to save the buildings, but another roof was alight to the left of the bakers this time. John Giddings felt his livelihood about to go up in smoke before the afternoon was out. He wanted to remove his stock, to try to salvage something, but the risk was too high, and the rain would damage the stock anyway. *If only the downpour were able to douse this red-hot blaze rather than just dampen the spread.*

Coming to investigate for himself, Reverend Howard Swinnerton let John know his father, at least, was safe at the Railway Arms. After a good hour or two of concerted effort with the buckets, it seemed the fire was out. The poor old baker had nearly lost everything in the inferno. The cobblers and butchers shops were water and smoke damaged, and the roofs needed attention, but they were salvageable. Thankfully, the small alleyway between his shop and the butchers had helped insulate the hardware store from the fierce heat. An exhausted but relieved John Giddings went to collect his father and his new wife and bring them back to their new home—the family home—which had been mercifully spared any serious damage.

He arrived at the Railway Arms, blackened and sweating heavily. Catching sight of the two of them, he weaved his way through the bunches of wedding guests who had also taken shelter, and across to where they were sitting.

"How about I get us all a gin to steady our nerves?" he offered.

Bess nodded, and his father insisted he help John carry the three drinks, shuffling behind, despite the son preferring him to stay safely seated. As the years progressed, his dear old pater was getting more and more unsteady.

John placed his order and was grateful the landlord, Mr Strickland, said the drinks were on the house to celebrate his nuptials earlier in the day. The groom gave him a hearty thank you for his generosity. Waiting to be served, George said in a hushed tone:

"I don't know how to tell you this—and it breaks my heart to do it, son—but that lovely young wife of yours loves you not. Her heart belongs to another. That's why she was so sullen during your ceremony."

John Giddings looked on, incredulous, and dismissed the idea promptly.

"Don't be ridiculous, Father. How could you possibly think that? I know our engagement has been short, and it will take time for Bess to grow to love me as I love her, but she did marry me this morning—not someone else."

Determined to make his point, George continued.

"It's young Harry Sutherland, Hamilton's gamekeeper. He's the one she lives for, not you. When you ran off to save the shop, I saw him holdin' her in his arms, bold as brass. For quite some time too, gazin' into each other's eyes. I've been on this earth long enough to know what that sort of look means."

With no more help needed by the shops, Harry too had just arrived, keen for a pint to quench his thirst. George nodded in his direction to John as he spoke, to reveal who his son's foe was.

John's face became more thunderous by the second, so angry that the landlord had to call him twice by name to let him know his drinks had been served. He looked down and took each glass of gin in rapid succession and quaffed it down in one. Mr Strickland looked on with consternation at his brazen show of greed, but John didn't care as his father divulged more of his observations.

"He must have thought everyone had gone to deal with the fire. He didn't reckon on me, with these tired old legs of mine, bein' forced to stay back at the lichgate, seein' that knave work on her affections. I thought he was goin' to kiss her, John. Grabbed her and pulled her right up close he did. They were almost toe-to-toe, talkin' sweet nuthin's no doubt."

With the gin soaking into his bloodstream, the forlorn groom planned to give Harry Sutherland a piece of his mind.

"You'll remember he turned up late to your ceremony and that he wasn't invited. And you must have noticed that wife of yours was in a trance during the entire service?"

John Giddings had heard enough. Across the busy alehouse, he could see Harry Sutherland stood at the far entrance, nursing a pint of beer. He shot across the room like a bullet, parting the crowd of drinkers in his wake like Moses parting the Red Sea. He aimed a punch at his adversary's face. Not being handy with his fists, it was only a glancing blow.

Like a cornered animal, Harry Sutherland fought back ferociously, his dropped pint glass smashing on the floor, carrying small shards of glass in the liquid as it spread on the tiles.

The rivals punched each other like two bare-knuckled fighters from the worst slum in London. Everyone in the pub turned to see what the commotion was. George and Bess looked on, distraught—for different reasons.

Full of rage, the substantial bulk of John Giddings lunged at Harry and wrestled him to the ground. The game-keeper had fallen awkwardly and hit his head on the floor with a sickening thud. As he tried to soften the land-ing, instinctively, Harry put his hands out. The right one landed on a big shard of glass, almost cutting the down to the bone. His left hand fared slightly better, but was still bleeding. The landlord tried to get close to the men to break up the fight, but couldn't get through the circle of onlookers. John grabbed his half-paralysed love rival by the hair and snarled, "Stay away from my wife!", then smashed his skull on the floor again, before he was dragged off by William Burridge, shocked by the ruth-lessness of the attack.

"Stop it. You'll kill the man," yelled Burridge. "Calm down."

Mr Strickland helped a dazed Harry Sutherland to his feet and held the two adversaries at arm's length for a few moments before ordering them to agree to put an end to their brutal violence. Given how bloodied Harry's hands were, shaking on it would be impossible.

Harry, wracked with guilt, earnestly said:

"The better man as won. You're her husband, not me. I will leave Woodborough and let you get on with your life together."

But that olive branch wasn't enough for John Giddings. *That gal-sneaker needs to be taught a bigger lesson.*

Instead of acknowledging the apology, with a shocking display of impropriety, the shopkeeper shoved Sutherland hard in the chest causing him to lose his balance again. The gamekeeper's long legs got tangled up with a stool, and he stumbled backwards, banging his temple hard on the arm of a wooden bench next to the door. Instantly, he lost consciousness as he landed on the tiles, with his sticky, dark blood oozing out from the wound mingling with the spilt beer and glass shards. The sickening blow had caused Harry's right eye to balloon up angrily and was caked shut with blood from the smaller lacerations on his face.

Seeing the grisly head wound, an anxious Mr Strickland yelled:

"He needs a doctor! Now! Before the lad pegs it."

Bess was horrified, embarrassed and heartbroken in equal measure, as a wooden cart promptly appeared outside, ready to take Harry to the doctor's office over on the opposite side of Woodborough. Mr Strickland took control of the situation and asked John to leave.

In disgrace, the three Giddings' left the pub, sensing the eyes of all the astonished, prying wedding guests burning a hole in their backs as they disappeared out of sight.

18

HAPPY FAMILIES

Back at the smoky shop, John Giddings opened all the windows to let in some fresh air. Bess was pleased to see the damage was mainly superficial. His beleaguered father struggled up to bed, too angry to be in the same room as 'that woman.' At first, the newlyweds said nothing and horrible silence filled the air for a good few hours.

Bess kept herself busy doing some cleaning, scrubbing the grate like Meg and Sarah had shown her when she first arrived at Walton Hall. *My muddy dress can't get any shabbier.* She sensed her menacing husband staring at her every move. Since the police had not visited to arrest him, she presumed that Harry was still alive.

After rehearsing his words a thousand times in his head, John Giddings stood up and walked over to his wife. He grabbed her by the shoulders to make her face him and then made his views on the day's events very clear, shouting:

"You are sweet on him, but you married me. How could you be so cruel? What was I? Second best? Someone to make do with? Someone to pay the bills? A meal ticket? Your route to escape the workhouse?"

He shook her violently as the words tumbled out of his mouth, which was foaming with fury. His teeth gnashed in front of her, like a rabid dog.

The strain had become all too much for Bess. She'd not eaten all day, had been chilled to the marrow in the rain, and worked tirelessly on housework to avoid the ire of her new husband. Exhausted, demoralised and shocked by the outburst, everything turned black, and she lost her balance. She slumped backwards and slid down the wall. A remorseful John picked up his bride, who was now out cold, and carried her to the rocking chair and gently placed her in it. *She's your wife. Few people marry for love, you fool. What makes you think Bess is so different?*

On hearing the almighty thump, George came downstairs as fast as his old knock-kneed legs could carry him. He found Bess slumped in the chair with his son stifling his snivelling, kneeling at her feet.

What with the chaos of the shop nearly burning down and finding out his catatonic bride was in love with another man, this was not how John Giddings had imagined his first day of married life to begin.

Thankful to see her breathing, George decided to take control.

"She can't stay there, John. She needs proper rest. Get her to bed. Your bed." He emphasised.

With a heavy heart, John Giddings picked up his limp bride, and took her upstairs, laying her down on the covers, still wearing her muddied and ragged white dress.

Our wedding will clearly not be consummated this evening, with her in this state. It was yet another blow to John Giddings' pride and his dream of finally being the man of the house.

Leaving Bess upstairs to sleep, the father and son returned to the sitting room and talked.

"She might have had her head turned by that gamekeeper fellow, but she is married to you, John. In the eyes of the law, you are one flesh now, and that gives you a much greater hold over her than he does. She will grow to love you; she just needs time. You are a good man, remember that. Your poor mother was not too enamoured with me, to begin with, and yet we had twenty good years together."

He saw sense in his father's reasoning. Yet he wondered if he would ever love Bess as he had imagined—on that joyous afternoon when Mrs Harvey first put forward the idea of matrimony. In the lonely years since the death of his mother, he had seen a glimmer of hope that love—closeness—would return to his life. A pretty, eligible young woman to become his bride and be company for him, what was not to like? Everything, it seemed at the moment—especially if the police got involved with the vicious beating he gave Sutherland.

Deciding to put his best foot forward and show his nurturing, rather than nasty side, John trekked upstairs with a big bowl of steaming hot stew a kindly neighbour had dropped off for them, hoping he could wake Bess. She would need to eat if she were to regain her strength.

After some decent rest, now Bess could be stirred from her deep slumber.

John fought his way around the door, trying to move it with his elbows and feet, as he steadied the stew, desperate not to spill it.

The atmosphere was awkward.

> "I brought you some food, Bess. I wish today could have been a different start for us. This animosity is awful. You married me, and we need to make a go of our union. We have no other option. We'll be alright. You'll see."

His compassion now was a complete contrast to the angry tirade of earlier. He was like a different person. Bess looked on his kindly face. There was a tenderness to his expression, something that she had seen lacking between her late father and Mrs Harvey. *Perhaps one day, I might have romantic feelings for him, like the ones I have—had?—for Harry?* She kept that idea to herself.

She propped herself up with both sets of pillows, and her husband's hand gently passed her the bowl. She was grateful for his sensitivity.

"I hope you don't mind, but I got your clean nightgown out of your travel case, Bess, in case you want to get changed out of that dress of yours. It's been through the wars a bit, hasn't it? It's there at the end of the bed. I'll give you some time to yourself. You take care now and eat that stew. It'll warm you up."

John kissed her gently on the forehead, smiled as he affectionately smoothed her ruffled hair, and then went back downstairs.

Half an hour later, Bess heard a knock on the door. Thinking it was John coming to revisit her, she beckoned her visitor in, only to find it was George. She felt the anxiety rise again.

"My son cares for you, and you will be a good wife to him in time. He has opened his home to you, and now is taking good care of you, as you will take good care of him. My spinster sister is gone. We need the company of a woman around the house. It warms the soul of the building. All I ask is that you are loyal to him and that you do your duty as a wife. A young bairn would mean everything to him."

He turned to leave. Bess blinked away some tears that were starting to form. She could cope with being pleasant with John, but the thought of everything that 'wifely duty' entailed was not pleasant, especially when she could only buy time for a day or so, before 'the inevitable' would have to happen.

It would be the next night for the consummation to take place. John Giddings made sure they bonded every night for a week in the marital bed in an attempt to erase Harry Sutherland from Bess's mind. It seemed, to John at least, that his plan was working.

19

THE AWKWARD ENCOUNTER

Feeling trapped of late, Bess yearned to escape the confines of the hardware store. She had stayed in a lot in an attempt to integrate herself more quickly into her new household. She told her husband she needed to visit Walton Hall because Meg had popped in to say a buyer had been found, and it would be one of her last few chances to see her family together.

John suspected that was probably a lie, but also felt it would be unreasonable to stop her from seeing her family before it was splintered and spread across the four corners of the kingdom. He was annoyed she couldn't be chaperoned during the visit, but he and his father needed to look after the shop.

Bess didn't care about Mrs Harvey, of course, but she was keen to find out how everyone else was faring and what plans they had.

"I'll be back soon, John", said Bess smiling reassuringly, before leaving for the hall.

She turned into the back lane up towards Hamilton House and thought she saw Harry further up the road, shuffling along, hunched over, his head still bandaged to cover the nasty wound he'd suffered at the hands of her husband. His palms were wrapped in thick dressings too.

As she dashed towards him, desperate to see how he was, she sensed Harry's feelings for her had changed after the fight. With his one unbandaged eye, he turned to see who owned the footsteps behind him, then his face fell. The atmosphere felt decidedly frosty.

Bess was horrified to see his battered face. Several days after the attack, he was still severely wounded. It seemed like the cuts had got infected by the looks of it.

"You keep away from me, Miss Harvey, or should I say, Mrs Giddings. You belong to another now. I nearly lost everything because of you. I can't see properly and I can't do my work around the estate. Lord Hamilton is furious. I'm returning to my cottage— Alone!"

He didn't want to be near her anymore. She was spoken for. Further, with his appearance, he felt ugly, unlovable and ashamed. A real man would have fought his corner bravely, not ended up an assault victim. Now, on the cusp of losing the eyesight in his infected eye, and his injured hands unable to handle a shotgun accurately, he was sure he would lose his job. *Who would want a steward unable to shoot straight at game—or challenge intruders effectively?*

Although his physical wounds might eventually heal, Harry felt the knife wound through his heart never would. He turned to walk away, but she followed, like his loyal work dog, Jasper.

"Bess, your return and your marriage has brought me nothing but trouble. Go back to your husband and start your new life."

"I don't want to! It's you I want, Harry. We must find a way to be together. John has such a cruel streak at times. I wish I'd dared to tell you I loved you when I first came back from boarding school. If only I'd not seen that servant. Mrs Harvey would have me marry a convict waiting to be transported if she could. She didn't care who I was with, unlike her own children—"

"So, you could have dropped your standards and married a poor man of the land like me, rather than your precious shopkeeper fellow. How lovely." He replied angrily.

At the top of his lungs, he decided to make his thoughts clear:

"Go away! I don't want another man's wife as my mistress. I'll get a good woman for myself. Understand?"

Devastated, Bess retaliated.

"Oh, I do, Harry. I won't bother you again. Have no fear of that. I'm not sweet on you anymore, don't you worry."

She turned towards Walton Hall, with him shouting after her:

"You're no good, Bess. You're cursed. Messing with my head like this. How I could have ever loved someone like you? Leave me be!"

His voice carried quite a distance in the breeze, so far that his stark comments were within earshot of the cobbler's wife, Mrs Greer, who had been picking flowers from the lane's lush hedgerows. She had hoped to add some cheer to their poor little shop after the fire.

A stunned Mrs Greer was astonished that a new bride could seek so openly to betray her husband, not yet married a month. She felt obligated to tell her fellow shopkeeper, John Giddings what she heard, word-for-word.

Bess didn't make it to Walton Hall. She was too upset. She regained her composure and came home the long way, giving her enough time to firmly fit her 'cheerful' mask once more. That night, she needed to keep the mask on as her husband took his pleasure yet again. It wasn't getting any easier.

20

LOVE, HONOUR AND OBEY

The next day, Bess decided to keep well clear of Harry Sutherland and make her new home at the hardware shop as comfortable as possible. She scrubbed the range, cleaned the floors, swept the back yard, tackled a mountain of laundry and made hearty meals for the family. Unaware of her recent secret liaison with Sutherland, it seemed to John that she was turning the corner and adjusting to her new household and husband.

Out of her upstairs bedroom window, Mrs Greer saw Bess pegging out some fresh laundry, smiling at her spouse when he came to see how she was managing. He held her hands for a while as he passed her some tea.

This falsified vision of domestic bliss irritated Mrs Greer tremendously. She had been fighting with her conscience since hearing the angry exchange between Bess and Harry in the lane. Seeing a decent man like Mr Giddings be taken in by this latest show of fake affection tipped her over the edge. She reasoned that if it were her, she would want to know if her husband had eyes for another woman, and took the opportunity to visit during the regular lull in custom between breakfast and lunch to confess what she had discovered.

Apologising to Mr Greer who was still busy trying to get parts of the shop back to normal after the fire, she said she had to pop out store for 'something'. He assumed she was attending to a task around the home, and waved her off.

An anxious Mrs Greer soon arrived at the doorway of the hardware store.

"Have you got time for a word, Mr Giddings?"

"Always for you, Mrs Greer," he smiled. "What can I get for you?" he enquired.

"In private, please? It's a delicate matter."

"Of course, Mrs Greer. It can be our secret." He replied, thinking she perhaps needed to ask for something on credit. *They must be struggling with the expense of making good their premises.*

Since Bess had come in to prepare some soup for lunch in the back, and his father was perched behind the counter in the showroom, the front of the shop by the pavement was the only vaguely suitable private place.

An out of earshot George was desperate to know what the matter might be and spent his time second-guessing what Mrs Greer would divulge. *I bet it's something to do with that girl. Sure as eggs is eggs.*

Outside the shop, Mr John Giddings straightened up his buckets and brooms to kill time as a couple of people walked past.

Then, after scanning up and down the street to see if the coast was clear, the shopkeeper asked:

> "What's on your mind, Mrs Greer?"

> "—It's that young wife of yours, Mr Giddings. I saw her talking with that chap you had—the incident with—in the Railway Arms."

His young face deepened with lines as he scowled angrily. *Not him again? What now?*

Recounting what she witnessed, she continued:

> "She must have been propositioning him because I heard him shout, 'Go away! I don't want another man's wife as my mistress.' Now, Mr Sutherland had clearly given her the brush off, but I got the sense that if he were to be more accommodating, she would run to his arms."

She leaned towards him and added in a whisper:

> "—and I think you know where that might lead."

John Giddings knew precisely where.

"Thank you for telling me, Mrs Greer. I appreciate your loyalty and discretion. There's not enough of that to go around at the moment," he complained as he shook Mrs Greer's hand to bid her farewell, then turned to go inside.

His father asked what the discussion was about that was so important they needed to slope off.

"Mr Greer needs some new tools for his cobbling business, to replace the ones damaged in the fire. Knives to trim the leather, glues, and the like. They need to get them on the tick since their takings have dropped off of late. They're proud people and good payers normally. It's hit them hard getting back on their feet."

"So, it wasn't a private matter about that wayward young bride of yours?"

"No!" was the hostile reply. I'll keep Mrs Greer's revelation to myself for now. What am I to do?

The evening meal that night had an intimidating tinge to it. Very little was said. George fell asleep in the chair after dining. John looked at the shop accounts. Bess resorted to her usual distraction of embroidery to spare her more anguish thinking about Harry.

At bedtime, Bess retired first, hoping to feign being asleep before her husband appeared. She got in her nightdress, then got into bed, trying to envelop herself in the blankets. Minutes later, her husband joined her.

He chipped away at the tightened covers encasing his wife, not in the mood to be spurned again. *I'll show her who she is to be with.*

It was clear she was still unhappy about his romantic advances, but as his wife, she had no choice but to comply. She turned away from him, desperate to indicate there would be no conjugal rights that evening.

"You can't push me away Bess. I'm your husband," he said insistently.

"It's not that. I have some good news." Turning over to look him straight in the eye, cradling his face tenderly in her hands, "I'm pregnant," she lied.

She took his hand and placed it on her belly, then kissed him passionately.

"Well, surely it's good that we still lay together, isn't it? It's good for the bairn. It'll feed it—"

"I'm terrified something might happen, John. It's my first child. What if I miscarry? I do love you and having your child—our child—means everything to me. Give me a few more days, for the baby to grow stronger. That's all I ask."

Disappointed, furious and confused, and not in the mood for an argument with his now expectant wife, John Giddings gave up his amorous chase of her that night. In fact, he would never have carnal knowledge of her flesh again. He would have to make do with hugs and kisses.

The following day, Bess was up bright and early, well before John could pursue her affections, and continued with her chores.

21

T IS FOR TEMPTATION

Although things had calmed down in the Giddings' household, Bess was starting to feel like a glorified slave at the hardware store. She was expected to be either working in the shop, doing the laundry in the backyard, preparing or cooking a meal, making beds, sorting out the privy. There was so much work to do; she had no reason, or opportunity, to leave the shop.

Her husband had asked the local shopkeepers to drop off any provisions they needed so he could keep an eye on her all day every day. He 'advised' her she mustn't exhaust herself on errands around the town now she was 'expecting'.

Whilst their relationship had become less rancorous over the past week since Beth's announcement of her faked pregnancy, the couple were indeed not the embodiment of marital bliss.

Bess was desperate to know what happened to Harry, her childhood sweetheart. *Was he recuperating, being looked after, or struggling alone?* She kept imagining running off together, to some distant country estate, pretending to be man and wife. Despite his recent rejection of her advances, she decided to feign illness to avoid attending the lengthy church service that Sunday. It was the perfect window of opportunity, and she was taking it. After seeing the two Giddings men walk out of sight, she put on one of her largest, frilled bonnets and turned her shawl inside out in a basic attempt to disguise her appearance. Then, she hurried to the gatekeeper's cottage with some bread and cheese in case Harry, in his isolated and incapacitated state, was struggling to eat properly. They say a *way to a man's heart is through his stomach, so I shall make sure he is fed.*

Bess felt responsible for Harry's plight. It was her jealous husband who had attacked him. It was her false presumption he was already married that stopped her wild streak from confessing how she felt. Even if they might never be together, she did want to atone for her mistakes at the very least. Looking behind her at regular intervals, she checked she wasn't being followed.

At the door of the small white cottage, she gave a loud, determined knock. A shocked and angry Harry slowly answered, still struggling because of his lingering, infected wounds. He looked in a terrible way.

"I told you before, didn't I? You're someone else's woman now. Why can't you just leave me alone, Bess?" said a defensive Harry.

"You know why. It's so lonely in that shop. John is a good man, but he doesn't fill my soul with joy as you do. Just seeing you makes me come alive. That's all I ask now, just to see you. Nothing else. I promise—I miss your friendship. You've been a rock to me over the years, and I to you, I believe." she implored.

The cottage was in desperate need of a good clean. Harry's injuries had left him somewhat incapacitated, and his short temper had alienated Lord Hamilton's servant girls who had stepped in to help before. They now avoided the place for fear of an ear-bashing. Bess looked for where to start first with the mess.

"You can stop that. You know where the door is. See yourself out."

Ignoring Harry's blunt request to leave, Bess began tidying the cottage. His possessions were strewn all over the place. The laundry was piled in a heap in the corner. The curtains were drawn. Beside the fire, the coal-scuttle was empty. The range was stone cold and had clearly not been in use for days. She asked:

"Have you been able to eat properly? I have some freshly baked bread and some cheese with me, if you'd like some?"

"Not for me, thanks. I'm fine," he replied with belligerence.

Harry's stomach rumbled so loudly at the mention of food, she knew he was lying. *Perhaps he's being dishonest about other feelings too?* Bess put a few slices and the block of cheddar on a plate and handed it to him. Their eyes met, and their hands were almost in touching distance as she reached over to him. *Why can't I just hate this woman? Life would be much easier.*

"Thank you," he said gruffly then chomped gratefully on the snack.

Bess carried on with the chores for a while in an attempt to regain Harry's trust. So close to him now, her mind was racing, her anguish building. Then, before she could stop herself, she blurted out her deepest thoughts, laying her heart on her sleeve one last time. *One last roll of the dice, Bess. You have to at least try.*

"I have persevered since the wedding to be a wholesome wife, but I just don't love Mr Giddings. I flinch with dread when he comes near me. It was all Mrs Harvey's idea. I was forced into it. He's kindly. He's pleasant. But something is missing. There's no— spark."

Harry started to worry as his compassion for her predicament was straying dangerously towards passion. *Steady, now. Remember the promise you made to yourself, Harry. Spare her feelings but move on.*

"I wish I'd not been so shy, Bess. Honestly, I do. I thought that the Harveys were looking for the ideal husband for you—not a lowly gamekeeper like me earning a few pounds a year. Besides, what can I offer you in a draughty old lodge like this? There's barely enough room for me. You're married, Bess. Face it. We're just not meant to be."

Bess looked at him solemnly.

"You've forgotten one important thing, Harry. I'm not a Harvey. Well, I was by name, I suppose, but I came from much humbler beginnings. Part of me is still the shepherdess' granddaughter, who spent half her life living at a remote cottage in the hillside by the colliery. An existence very much more like yours now. I don't belong in a hall with fancy parlours, dining rooms and landscaped gardens—I don't belong above a shop either. I have lived there but because I have no choice. Neither is my home—being with you—feels like home," she beseeched.

Harry looked on from a distance, desperately not wishing to get involved with a married woman for nothing good would come of it.

"You can forget that talk, Miss. I am looking for jobs elsewhere. I'll be nothing to you soon. You've got to make that marriage work—you'll have a much better life."

Feeling agonisingly alone, now with the thought of Harry leaving the Hamilton estate too, she put her head in her hands and began to cry.

Seeing his lovely Bess so dejected cut deep into him. He wanted to comfort her like he did when he first found her, the lost ragamuffin in the boathouse but ignored his brain. *Your mind's playing tricks on you, Harry Suther-land. You've got to be strong.*

She turned to look at him, and walked over slowly, holding his gaze firmly in hers, until she was within arm's reach. There she waited, still staring at him intently, with the occasional sniff. She left him in no doubt about her intentions. He might have looked like a lout, all cut and bruised, but underneath it all, he was still her dear old Harry.

He put his arms around her sad little sobbing body, hoping that the warmth and strength of his own would comfort her as it had done in the past.

In an instant, the spark between them was reignited, and there was to be no turning back. Temptation took over.

"Bess, there is no one else for me. I am tired of being lonely. I need the female touch. Your touch."

He swept her up in his arms and carried her to his bed as she began to loosen her dress to let him know he could have what he wanted. A new chapter was about to start in their relationship.

Afterwards, an affectionate Bess felt blissfully relaxed, resting her head on his chest, hearing his steady heartbeat. A heart that beat for her and her alone. After the years of wait, she wanted to stay there forever like that.

Alas, the inevitable march of time was to sour the moment. The Giddings would be back from church soon, and she had to flee.

"I wish with all my heart I could stay," she confided. "I am most definitely yours. But for now, these secret meetings will be all we have until we have a better plan. You best get looking for new work, Harry Sutherland. I'm quite partial to the idea of living in a cottage again," she said mischievously.

"Wait for me, Harry, I will be back very soon."

With that, and a final spine-tingling kiss, she got dressed and hurried back home before her absence was detected.

Things will be very different next time I see Harry Sutherland; I just know it. She didn't know then that their next romantic encounter would be days away—and very different in tone.

22

THE CHEERFUL HOUSEWIFE

John Giddings found it curious that his wife was in good spirits after being quite ill earlier in the day. Bess was brighter in the shop and took on even the most gruelling of chores with a cheerful vigour. She was like a new person. He decided she was adjusting to motherhood and perhaps the acute morning sickness she'd complained of had passed.

Bess felt it beneficial to appear trustworthy and helpful to avoid arousing any suspicion that she had enjoyed her clandestine morning union with Harry.

With her husband organising the stock at the front of the shop, George Giddings asked:

"What have you got to be happy about?"

"It's motherhood, George. It makes me positively glow. I can't wait for us to live together as a proper family. John cannot wait to be a father."

Her suspicious father-in-law didn't believe a word of it. He'd not heard her struggle with morning sickness in the privy or seen the evidence in the chamber pot. *She seems to wander off into her own thoughts far too much, probably daydreaming about that gamekeeper. John's complained that she's decided meeting his physical needs has to be put on hold, for now at least, because of the pregnancy. There was the private chat with Mrs Greer. She never came in to pick up those 'important' supplies. It all points to one thing—lies.*

Sensing an atmosphere as he came into the shop, John nipped the hostilities in the bud muttering in his father's ear out of range of Bess's:

"She's one of the family now—and in the family way, Father—you have to accept that. Let me handle this. Arguing is not going to solve anything."

George got away with giving him a phoney smile; not confident his son would 'handle' it at all.

One day seemed to blend into another, each following a similar pattern. Since they didn't have anything new to say to each other, cooped up all day every day, the three of them busied themselves tidying the shop and serving the customers, all pulling together, albeit superficially.

John Giddings finally began to think that his marriage had not been a terrible mistake. He had conveniently convinced himself Mrs Greer was mistaken, and her observation was mere tittle-tattle. Keen not to alienate Bess, who seemed to be warming to him at last with her frequent caresses and smiles, he respected her wishes about not stressing the baby. Equally, not wanting to live the celibate life of a monk, he said within a week, it would be time for her to start meeting his physical needs again. Bess was not looking forward to the prospect.

The next day, early in the morning, Bess was outside in the courtyard, getting a bucket of coal to get the range heated up to prepare breakfast. She bent down, almost double, straining as she pushed a small metal scoop into the coal sack to get at the last of the brittle shiny blackness within. Suddenly, she had an extremely peculiar feeling in her belly and made her way to the privy. It was close to the house, and the stench from it often wafted into the shop if the breeze was blowing in the right direction. The smell always made her nauseous, more so today.

In the gloom, she put her hands on the wooden seat either side of the hole and fought (and failed) not to vomit.

In that time, her father-in-law had come downstairs to see if the chickens in the yard had laid any eggs for their breakfast. He heard the retching then saw a pale-looking, disorientated Bess tentatively leave the privy, wiping her mouth on her sleeve.

"So, it's not a lie then—you are with child?" he chided, glad that for once Bess was not leading his son a merry dance again.

Yes, I am. But it must be Harry's, not my husband's. Panic retook root in Bess's mind.

She went inside to make a cup of tea to take the foul taste out of her mouth. She collapsed feebly on the rocking chair; it's unsteady motion not helping at all. George Giddings shuffled through the sitting room, predictably, to tell his son she was definitely expecting. *At least this will make it easier to keep John away from me. There's real proof I am unwell at times. How am I going to tell Harry? How will he react? Everything's such a mess.*

In the shop, a proud John Giddings was delighted to know that the pregnancy was really progressing. So far, there had been very little outward sign. He was starting to wonder if Bess had used it as a ruse to keep him away, but now with fatherhood on the horizon, he felt his love for his expectant wife begin to blossom fully.

Bess looked incredibly pale. She was clammy, and her lips were almost blue. Popping in to check up on her, John squeezed her hand tenderly and stroked the back of it to try to soothe her discomfort, not realising the guilt was making her feel worse. She looked like she would retch again at any moment. George filled the range with the coal she'd collected and sat the empty scuttle next to the rocking chair, just in case it was needed in an emergency.

Wishing he could wave a magic wand to make her nausea better, but knowing he couldn't, John Giddings reconfirmed his promise to himself not to pressure her into marital relations, until she looked better.

The smitten husband helped Bess up to bed and pulled the covers back, so it was easier for her to get in. The empty scuttle followed the couple and was placed next to the bed by George in case of another emergency.

Lying on her back, John put his hand on her belly and kissed her. Then he went back downstairs to help his father with the shop. Bess felt trapped again by the sickness and the smothering attention John was giving her. *How on earth am I going to cope with the pressure of secretly carrying another man's child to full-term? Running away with Harry, though ludicrous is starting to make more sense, especially now.* She felt as crushed being at the mercy of the tragic hand of fate as her father had done by the rubble at the colliery.

23

A PROBLEM SHARED IS
A PROBLEM DOUBLED

For the next couple of days, Bess rested, apart from preparing simple meals, done mainly to prove her loyalty to her husband—since her body was firmly out of bounds. John and George did their best to keep the house functioning.

One good thing about the terrible symptoms was that Bess was allowed to get some fresh air to help with the nausea. John felt the smell from the gruesome privy in the backyard was not good at the best of times, let alone for his wife in her current condition.

Guessing she was a few weeks into her real pregnancy, she decided to risk going to see the real father, Harry. She told her husband she was going to pick some flowers and herbs from around the green and churchyard to make a posy to make their bedroom smell sweeter and look more welcoming.

John paid for a young lad, Mrs Greer's son Arthur, to follow Bess, not necessarily to spy upon her, but to be on hand if she were to feel ill and collapse whilst out walking. She still looked quite pale, and her sleep was terrible.

As a smokescreen, she headed off in the direction of where she said she was going, then took her detour. As Bess walked along the lane; the young boy followed behind doing his utmost not to be detected. She was unlikely to spot him as she was far too busy preparing what she would say to Harry. Arthur wondered why she wasn't heading in the direction Mr Giddings had said she would. *I can't exactly go and ask her, can I?*

She arrived at the cottage, exhausted from the walk, and went inside, making it extremely difficult for Arthur to spy on her. He made his approach creeping from bush to bush as quietly as possible until he could sit near an open window.

"How are you doing, Bess? You look weary. Come and sit down. Rest."

Harry's wounds were nearly all healed now, but the extensive damage to the ligaments in his hands still gave him problems with his work.

Arthur heard the noise of two people sitting down on the edge of a bed, the creak of the metal bedstead unmistakable. His eyes began to widen at the impropriety of it.

"Are you all right?" he asked, stroking her cheek softly, noticing she felt a little clammy.

"Yes—and—no", she replied cryptically.

"The reason why I look out of sorts—"

Silenced again with fear, she inhaled deeply to give herself Dutch courage, as she had at her wedding ceremony. Letting the words tumble out as her lungs emptied, she quietly revealed:

"It's because I'm pregnant. Pregnant with your child."

She closed her eyes in a futile attempt to soften the blow of what Harry was bound to say next.

"How can you be sure? How do you know it's not Mr Giddings'?"

"Because I've not been with him for a while, Harry. I lied to him. I told him I was expecting ages ago and I was terrified I would miscarry if we were to lie together. Being an honourable man, and with his sister dying in childbirth, he respected my request. Back then, I wasn't pregnant. But I am now—after my last visit here. I have terrible sickness in the morning, and I've had no monthly visit since we—"

"I don't know what you want me to say," said a stunned Harry after a long silence. "You're another man's wife, and now you're carrying my child. There is no way we can be together. We'd be the talk of Woodborough. Are we supposed to elope to Gretna Green or something? I mean, I was looking for other jobs before we—" he tailed off.

"Still. This is a disaster." His harsh response cut Bess to the bone.

"Are you not happy that you are to be a father?"

"Not really, Bess! I've always wanted you; you know that. But now you're carrying my child. And you have a husband. This is all wrong."

Outside, Arthur was mesmerised, listening to the secret lovers' conversation. This was not what he expected to happen either.

"I asked you last time, what's to stop us running away, Harry? What if you got a job in another distant estate? No one would know us. Perhaps tell people that we're married already."

Harry was silent, looking at his damaged hands as he nervously clenched and unclenched his fists.

If I don't get better, we're not going anywhere. No landowner wants a crippled gamekeeper who can't shoot straight. And we'd be poor as anything if I settled for general labouring.

Bess gently touched his face with her hand and tried to kiss him, but he moved away. Undeterred, she leaned closer.

Arthur, peering through the foliage of his hiding place, then via a small window, saw her make a move on Harry.

What if we did run away? We wouldn't be the first? Surely, we can work something out if we really wanted it? Temptation and opportunity made poor Harry's muddled mind and body light up with desire.

And then, unable to control himself any longer, a confused Harry Sutherland yielded and turned his head towards Bess and kissed her back.

"Let me think, Bess, let me think," he whispered in her ear before their entwined bodies gently sank down towards the eiderdown and out of view.

The boy had seen and heard everything that he needed to. He edged away quietly then ran along the lane, desperately working out how to handle breaking the news back at the hardware shop.

Once there, the wheezing and breathless young boy furtively recounted what he had seen to an increasingly furious John Giddings. The shopkeeper pressed a few coins into the boy's hand and thanked him for his efforts then turned him around to usher him out of the shop in double-quick time. He flipped the cardboard sign in the door to 'closed' and went to talk to his father. Mrs Greer's observation had been the smoke of this ugly business with his wife. Young Arthur had just seen the fire.

"What now? Why are you shutting the shop?" asked George, seeing him seething yet again.

"Come through to the back, now!"

Barely pausing for breath as he ranted, John Giddings finally boiled over.

"Seems that lovely wife of mine is pregnant with another man's child. Arthur caught her cavorting with him at his cottage this afternoon when she was supposed to be gathering plants for a posy for our bedroom. Talking of running off, and the like. How could she betray me like this? Who does she think she is? I thought I'd made it clear when we had the fight in the pub, that his advances were not welcome. And yet it was in vain. Like a pair of rabbits, they've been seeing each other behind my back, making a right fool of me. And now she is having his child. She's kept me away from her for a good while now. It must be his."

In his fury, he smashed his fist into the plump padding at the back of the rocking chair. The chair almost toppled over. He'd struck it exactly where Bess's belly would be if she were sitting there.

John added:

"You will say nothing of this, Father. Let me deal with it. Nothing. Do you understand?"

George nodded. He had no idea how to solve his son's catastrophic marital problems anyway.

Not long after, Bess came back with a small bunch of herbs and flowers, like nothing had happened, cheerily walking into the sitting room.

But she was fooling no one. As soon as she set down what she had picked, John Giddings, master of the house, ordered her upstairs, roughly shoving her towards the steps.

A terrified Bess looked back at him as he bellowed:

"It's time to talk."

He slammed the bedroom door behind them. Bess felt like a prisoner.

24

THE REPRIMAND

Out of view and earshot in the upstairs room, the furious husband slapped his wife across the face. A terrified Bess stumbled and fell. *What have you become, John Giddings?* A sense of intense guilt now mingled with his fury.

"I know the child isn't mine, Bess. Your charade can stop. You need to learn a lesson, you deceitful woman."

Bess looked at him. *What's going on? How could he have found out? He needed to work in the shop all afternoon?* She was baffled—and very afraid.

"You see, young Arthur Greer, the cobbler's son, followed you. I asked him to. I was worried you might be taken ill on your walk. I feel so stupid for caring now. He said he saw you with another man. That gamekeeper fellow. Even lay on his bed with him, like you were his wife! You told him, he's the one who owns that bun in the oven!" he yelled.

He paced about, full of rage.

"Don't try and deny it. His mother, Mrs Greer, saw you propositioning him too, down by the lane, a few days ago. Goodness knows how long you wanted to carry on with him behind my back."

He stood over her, menacingly, as she crawled towards their bed, trying to pull herself up off the floor. He heaved her head up by the hair and forced her to look at his furious face, spitting out the words:

"You've betrayed me. The lies. The infidelity. I hate you. You make me sick to the stomach when I look at you. I wish I'd never met you. Seems widowed Mrs Harvey, not hiding away at our wedding has cursed us after all. I don't know who's the more spiteful, you—or her?"

After hearing the almighty thud and the tell-tale heavy footsteps, an anxious George Giddings walked upstairs, listening as he went. When his curiosity got the better of him, he opened the door. Shocked, he saw his son, a solid wall of muscle, his breath hissing rhythmically through his flaring nostrils like a bull about to charge. A petrified, hysterical Bess was still crumpled on the floor.

"Think of the child, John," he bellowed.

"Why should I care? It's not my child. It belongs to that hapless gamekeeper fellow, Harry Sutherland, doesn't it?"

His son raised his hand to hit her again.

"John. John! We don't want you up for murder. Calm down. Please!"

"I'm going to see that lothario and make it clear to him that his presence is no longer welcome in Woodborough. I'm sure he knows that anyway but reinforcing the principle will do no harm. She is my wife, and he will keep away."

Bess started to groan as she hoisted her way onto the bed, then rolled from side to side in acute distress, clutching her belly.

The stress of carrying another child, living with a man she didn't love, losing her father, being separated from her half-siblings, caused a weakened and agitated Bess to finally give up struggling. She collapsed on the bed and sobbed.

John Giddings didn't know what to do for the best. He hated what his life had become. He imagined throwing Bess down the stairs like a rag doll to put an end to his heartbreak, but the fear of the punishment for such a devilish crime stopped him. *What if I tied my shoelaces together and followed her? Stop it, John, you're talking nonsense.*

He looked at her as she lay in bed, exhausted. He dearly wished for things to be different, but they were not going to be. Dismayed, he couldn't see a sensible way forward.

He watched over her as she slept, more to keep out the way of his father's snide comments than any loyalty to her.

A few hours into his bedside vigil, Bess's eyes flickered open. Self-preservation was the order of the day. She wracked her brains for the best thing she could think of that her husband would want to hear.

"I've learned my lesson, John. I will never see Harry Sutherland again. Just as Mr Harvey raised me, so too you can raise this little nipper. We'll get by, you'll see—"

She trailed off realising she was wasting her breath. Her husband was not interested in any attempt at reconciliation. If fact, he got up and left the room, slamming the door behind him.

Bess hoped that word would get around about their failing marriage and the gossips in the neighbouring shops would let Meg and Sarah know to visit. Through them, she could perhaps get a message to Harry and convince him not to leave without her. *We have to escape together—it's my only chance. I am going to be under lock and key here.*

Downstairs, John Giddings was out of his depth, wondering what to do for the best. *For now, I will grin and bear it until I can come up with a better plan.*

25

FUN AT HARVEST TIME

The mood in the shop at the weekend was brightened by Woodborough's Harvest Festival, one of the most popular fêtes held in the county, with lots of stalls, snacks and entertainers. The children loved to play games like hook the duck, cover the coin and hopscotch. In the church, hymns were sung to celebrate the bounty, with no one needing the hymn sheet to finish 'We plough the fields and scatter' and 'All things bright and beautiful.' The highlight for Bess was always a competition to be judged by the vicar on who had made the best corn dolly.

The couple had decided to attend in an attempt to hide their marital discord. It was time to show a united front. Things would only get worse as Bess was confined in the later months of her pregnancy. Tongues were already starting to wag that the marriage was troubled, especially after talk of the altercation in the pub between John and Harry became common knowledge, plus the newlyweds were seldom seen together in public. Nobody, yet, had quite worked out how violent the new husband was behind closed doors.

George Giddings decided not to attend, saying he felt a little under the weather but insisted they still go. *A day out together away from the shop will do them good. Might even sort themselves out a bit? It can't make things worse.*

Wearing their best clothes, the couple walked onto the High Street. John took his wife's arm and laid it over his, so at least she had physical support from him if nothing else. *And I can stop her running over to him. She's that brazen. I'm sure she'd rub my nose right in it if she saw him. Can't use my fists in public again, can I?* They walked together towards the green near the market square where most of the stalls were erected.

He knew people were whispering as soon as they had passed, but the best way to silence those rumours was to show that they were a happy couple. As a plan, it seemed to be working.

Beth squeezed her husband's arm before trying to free herself. John Giddings looked down at her, suggesting woe betide her if she was off to see him. *She has proved she cannot be trusted for one second.*

"Look, there's Meg. I must talk to her. I want to know what's happening at Walton Hall. The last buyer fell through at the eleventh hour, so they need to start the process again. She'll be out of a job once that house is sold. And I want to make sure she's all right. She's always been good to me. Will you wait for me?"

Reluctantly, John Giddings agreed.

"If you must. I need to speak to the carpenter about some new display shelves for the shop and a few other odd jobs. I shall talk to him while you speak to Meg, I can see him standing in front of his workshop touting for business as usual. Let's meet here in a few minutes?"

He gave her a stern look with his eyes making it clear that deviation from that plan would be punished. *She knows better than to defy me again.*

"Well, look at you, Miss, I mean Mrs Giddings. You're positively blooming. Married life clearly suits you."

Without thinking Bess replied:

"I wish I felt like that, Meg." *What about the united front?* Quickly, she added, "I am not so good in the mornings," then stroked her abdomen.

"Oh! You're expectin' so soon! Well, congratulations, Bess! A little Giddings on the way. You must be made up! You'll be a proper little family then. How wonderful. I'm sure the sickness will pass in time."

Meg wasn't a tell-tale by any stretch, but Bess felt it would be helpful for more people to know she was pregnant—it would make it more difficult for John to throw her out if it came to it, for one thing.

"Tell me about Walton Hall. It seems to have been for sale for a very long time?"

"Well, Miss, I must tell you, sellin' the mine did prove tricky for Mrs Harvey and Master Richard. Thankfully, Mr David has been a blessing. I don't know what they would do without him. The colliery is sold now, but it is gone for less than they hoped. They accepted an offer for the hall, but they didn't do much checking. The buyer couldn't afford it in the end, so they are lookin' again. I am sure it will be sorted soon. The money from the mine will cover Mrs Harvey's bills for quite a while to come. I have no idea what Sarah and I will do when the time comes to leave, Miss. Still, we're survivors. Anyway, enough of that doom and gloom."

Suddenly feeling a little sick again, Bess didn't feel able to wait for Mr Giddings to come back from the carpenters.

"Meg, would you mind waiting and telling my husband I have had to return to the shop. I'm feeling queasy again. He is meeting me back here in a few minutes after he's popped to see the carpenter. Ask him to meet me at the shop, please?"

Bess looked pallid and kept swallowing every few seconds trying to control the nausea, making it easy for Meg to agree. She kept an eye on her as the weary young mother wobbled back to the hardware store.

Barely five minutes after leaving, John Giddings returned close to the meeting point, seeing Meg stood on her own with Bess nowhere to be seen. With her back to him, Meg was oblivious to his presence.

That wretched woman has gone to see him again. She must have. Everyone comes to the Harvest Festival. Now, where is he? It's time for a piece of my mind since my fists didn't get him to stay away before.

Too angry to ask Meg where Bess was, he made his way around the square, looking for her at all the stalls.

Approaching the shop, Bess was stunned to see George Giddings through the display window looking particularly unwell. She saw him staggering about the shop floor, moving stock around, trying out a new window display idea the men had discussed earlier in the week.

She thought he must have overexerted himself. There was far too much for an old man to move on his own. She was right in her assumption. George's knees buckled, and he toppled over like a felled pine.

"I was just trying to help John," he croaked feebly, as she checked on his condition.

With his head lolling about and his breathing shallow, Bess decided he needed to see a doctor.

She raced out of the door, forgetting her own queasy incapacity and yelled:

"Quick, get the doctor. It's my father-in-law, George. Quickly!"

Hearing the plea, Mr Greer the cobbler, offered to go.

The collapsed man, writhed on the floor in agony, clutching his belly, in too much pain to speak.

Within minutes, help had arrived. By that time, John had seen the commotion and had gone to investigate. His father was on the floor, lying on his side to ease his breathing. There was a pool of vomit, and he'd lost control of his bowels. His heart was racing. He looked like he had a fever coming on.

"Judging by the symptoms," Dr Croft said grimly, "it looks like cholera."

George Giddings was already unresponsive. The blue death seldom spared the elderly.

26

NURSE BESS

Just the word cholera struck the fear of God into the heart of the Giddings'. Those old enough remembered the first ravages of the pestilence in the 1830s. Another wave had been bringing death to the nation since 1846.

George was cleaned up as best as possible then taken upstairs for some privacy. He was delirious, and his eyes were rolling in his head. His tongue was lolling about in his mouth, which had become terribly dry. He kept clutching his abdomen and contorting and was obviously in a lot of pain.

For hours John and Bess watched over him, unable to do anything to help except spoon a few drops of laudanum into his mouth to reduce the pain—when he would accept it. Dr Croft had prescribed thirty drops a day, mixed with oil of peppermint and chalk. It would ease the aching at the very least.

"It's best you keep away, Bess. I don't want you and the bairn being struck down. You've been so sickly yourself recently. Go downstairs. Wait for me there. I'll be down soon."

It was the first thoughtful thing John Giddings had done for her in quite a while. Bess did as she was told and went to sit in the rocking chair, trying to soothe her nerves.

Later that night, she was woken with another fearful thud in the household. John had collapsed, weakened with the same disease that had struck his father. Bess was petrified she was going to catch it. She wondered if they had both eaten something contaminated while she had stuck to simple watery soups because of the morning sickness.

She called at the cobbler's shop and asked Mr Greer to help her get John into his bed.

Doctor Croft was called again who provided more of the chalky painkiller mixture. He promised to recommend to the Guardians that the premises be whitewashed and disinfected, and a barrel of tar and vinegar be burned to cleanse the air within and around the house.

Until dawn, Bess divided her time looking after her two patients, doing her best to make sure there was fresh air in the rooms. It was the only precautionary measure available. They were both suffering from bouts of intense sickness and diarrhoea. Keeping the sheets clean was not a realistic option. She left them lying there in their own filth, distressed by their rapid decline. They both looked frail—as if the Lord might take them at any moment.

The shop remained closed that day. It was pointless opening with no customers forthcoming. Everyone on the High Street was aware of the crisis. People were fearful of catching the awful disease that had struck down the two men, and decided to keep well away.

The only visitor was Doctor Croft, who solemnly told Bess to brace herself. They were both unlikely to survive the day. It was true she had gone to live with them out of necessity and duty rather than choice, but still, the news was a terrible blow.

She divided her time between checking on each of her patients, and then sat downstairs, to try to distance herself from the danger.

Although the closed sign was prominently displayed, someone decided to hammer at the door so loudly she felt the glass might shatter. *Who might that be? Please not Harry—.* With relief, she saw it was her brother, Richard. He looked puzzled that the usually thriving little shop was closed.

She unlocked the door. As it opened, the little shop bell rang out.

"Good morning, Richard. Do come in. I haven't got long though. Both Mr Giddings and his father are ill."

"Oh. I didn't know. Nothing serious, I hope. If my visit is inconvenient, I can call back?"

Bess chose not to say anything and hinted with a brave but hopeful facial expression instead. *Best not to worry him with the truth. He's got enough to deal with. I'll tell him to go as soon as he's passed on the message.*

Richard shared his news that he and Mrs Harvey had finally managed to sell Walton Hall, and the family would be moving imminently. He explained.

"Mama is going to start afresh, in a small cottage near the rest of the Carlyles."

"Nell is doing well with her teaching, although her engagement has fallen through. I suspect young Mr Carlyle and his parents have found out that we're not the family we used to be. He is looking for a new bride—a wealthier one. For now, she can lodge, but she'll need to get herself hitched and out of there soon."

"Oh poor, Nell. She was so happy, and now she's got to start again."

"I do worry about Meg and Sarah, of course. Mama's new cottage is too small for them. None of the Harveys or Carlyles require help at present. Perhaps they can help here, Bess? Could you at least put a roof over their head for a few nights while they find new work? They have been looking in the paper for new opportunities, but so far in vain."

Bess looked noncommittal, which puzzled Richard.

"They can help you tend to the Giddings' while they regain their strength? After all, they cared for you when you first arrived. They are good people."

"I might be able to do something, but who would want to live here with the blue death sweeping through the house."

"You mean—?"

Bess nodded gravely.

"Oh, Bess."

Keen not to develop the deadly disease, he reluctantly left her to cope alone. A fearful Bess opened more windows and carried on disinfecting their home.

27

THE HUNT

Bess continued to nurse the two men. George seemed to be rallying a little. John, however, was still in a perilous condition.

As she nursed her father-in-law, he regained sufficient consciousness for her to broach the subject of Meg and Sarah moving in temporarily to help with their care.

His cruel streak ruled his thinking still. *That selfish girl might want to ignore the fact she's carrying another man's child, but I will not. We owe her no favours.* Her request was declined.

Although barely able to lift a cup to his mouth, he still saw fit to order Bess around. Open the curtains. Close them. Bring some extra blankets. Take them away. Change the sheets. Bring food and drinks—that would be left untouched.

John Giddings had not been conscious now for some time and Bess was anxious about him. With intense reluctance, she confided in his father.

He decided it would be prudent to call the doctor again.

Whilst she went the short distance to go and fetch Doctor Croft, her husband was finally taken by the reaper; his suffering over.

Bess didn't know what to make of the matter. It felt like a huge burden had been lifted. *Am I glad he's dead? Maybe not glad—but relieved? How am I going to tell his father? And who will look after him? I suspect the responsibility will fall to me?*

She asked the doctor to go and break the news to George Giddings. That, at least, she might be spared from. She didn't have the heart to tell him, knowing how close they were. She felt that he would take the news better from a professional, then a daughter-in-law he loathed.

Listening outside the door, she heard the conversation play out.

"I want to see my son," said the bereft father, but the medical advice was that he was too weak to withstand it.

Doctor Croft called into the funeral director on the way back to his office and had the body promptly removed, as was the way with infectious diseases. His corpse would be buried within hours; his bed stripped and burned. The

Guardians would supply some replacement fresh sheets and mattresses. Bess had a terrible night's sleep, tossing and turning in the rocking chair. There was no time to contemplate widowhood with her father-in-law still clinging to life, in need of constant nursing.

Two days later, against all the odds, a cantankerous George Giddings could get out of bed.

Although he was too ill to come downstairs, he sat on a small armchair that had been put next to the window for him. He stayed there for a few hours. The view outside provided some gentle entertainment for him as he continued to recuperate.

Livid that his son was dead though, he took his feelings out on Bess. *She probably smothered him, knowing her. Never loved him, did she?*

Intense arguments flared up with increasing regularity.

"Leave this shop. You have no right to it. I have John's will, written before you had that farce of a marriage. You're not mentioned. None of this is yours, so you can forget any designs you have on my shop."

Bess knew wives inherited their husbands' property on their death. This paperwork that George spoke of seemed very convenient.

"Show me!" Bess demanded, but George refused, stating she would probably destroy the all-important piece of paper.

Furious, she fled downstairs to get away from him and pondered what her next move should be.

There must be some papers left somewhere. She didn't believe George had the foresight to get John's will and hide it somewhere in his room. He had suddenly collapsed on the day of the Harvest Festival. Surely the papers would still be with their shop's other important records, safely filed away, not randomly separated out.

She started to hunt around the shop, looking in every nook and cranny where it might be but drew a blank. The large pile of papers in a chest in the sitting room had yielded nothing, nor the wooden box by the shop counter. None of the drawers in the house brought any joy either. Bess collapsed in her rocking chair with frustration.

She had barely sat down when there was a knock at the door. It was Meg and Sarah who had come to pass on their condolences about her late husband.

> "How are you coping Miss? It must have been an awful shock, so soon after your wedding and all? And you with his child on the way too." consoled Meg.

Bess's thoughts returned to running away with Harry. There had been no chance to see him for quite a few days now. She had no idea how he was feeling. *Once again, I have the chance to be with him, and it is denied by fate.*

> "I'll survive. As you know, it's not the first time I have been forced to start again." Bess smiled forlornly.

"While we're here, Miss, is they anything we can do? Make up those new beds? Help with more disinfecting? With the Harveys packed and ready to leave any day now, there is little for us to do at the hall."

"Do you know I think there is something you can help with—" said Bess, and invited them both in.

She took the simmering kettle off the range and made a pot of tea, then explained her predicament about the missing will.

"We'll leave no stone unturned, Miss. We'll be quiet as church mice lookin' for them papers. Mr Giddings won't even know we're 'ere. We know 'ow to be discrete—" reassured Meg. Sarah nodded and gave a compassionate smile.

Bess took the opportunity to visit Woodborough's only solicitor. If someone else were to be storing the will, it had to be him. She had seen some commercial documents with his name on them. *Presumably, the Giddings' may have taken avail of his services for will provision too?* The only thing was that the solicitor was Mr Edward Mortimer. Having rejected his proposal earlier in the year, she felt the awkwardness build as she walked towards the office. *Needs must, Bess. Talk to the man. You have nothing to lose.*

Fortunately, when she arrived, Mr Mortimer was not seeing a client and was able to talk to her straight away.

The atmosphere was tense. Clearly, he remembered his spurned offer of marriage, and now here was Bess Giddings, asking about inheriting her dead husband's estate, barely weeks after their wedding.

The portly solicitor searched in vain through all the papers for the Giddings' household, but there was no trace of a will. Trying to help, Bess asked:

"Do you remember helping my late husband with wishes? He might have used another legal practice? Maybe that's why it's missing."

"I see so many people, Mrs Giddings. I daren't say for sure."

Sensing her despair, Edward Mortimer promised to keep looking and would come and see her, if he found anything.

"I must warn you—I don't hold out much hope for your quest."

"Thank you for your assistance, Mr Mortimer. You have been most helpful. I must get back and tend to my father-in-law."

Feeling dejected, she returned to the hardware store.

In the meantime, George Giddings was now strong enough to come downstairs, and a blazing row developed when he found the two servants' rifling through the shop and his daughter-in-law missing.

"You won't find what you're looking for. I've hidden it." snarled the old man. "This shop is rightfully mine. That villainous woman won't get a penny. You mark my words."

The two ladies looked astounded at the old man's spiteful outburst.

28

THE FIGHT FOR SUPREMACY

The angry, stand-up row had taken a lot out of the sickly old man. Bess, on her return, had no option but to reluctantly help him upstairs to bed, supporting his arm around her shoulder. It was the last thing either of them wanted to do.

She got him into bed and offered to keep him company, not because she thought that it would help him, but she knew that as soon as he was asleep, she would have a chance to search his bedroom and look for the wretched will he kept alluding to.

George Giddings complained bitterly, but in vain. It didn't take long for the weakened old man to slip into a slumber. Bess looked through his bedside drawers. *Nothing.* She lightly slid her hand around the edge of the mattress. *Nothing.* She peeked under the small rug next to his bed.

Nothing. She even raised a loose and squeaky floorboard. There was no paperwork to be found.

Wracked with a sense of defeat, she returned downstairs and found the two servants still doing everything possible to look around the property for the elusive piece of paper.

All of a sudden, Meg gave a shout.

"Quick, Miss. Come 'ere! Look! Look!"

Bess hurried into the central area of the shop and found Meg holding a false base panel that had been fitted inside the wooden shop counter. She was stood where the carpenter had been working on his last visit.

The large empty space at the base of the counter turned out to be an excellent hiding hole for secreting things away. To Bess's delight, there were several stacks of papers bound with ribbon, together with a few valuables lying below that; a watch and some jewellery. Meg had opened a curious black velvet bag. It contained a large stack of five-pound notes and a sizeable quantity of gold sovereigns. Clearly, it had been used as some sort of safe to store the Giddings' valuables and shop takings.

Bess studied each document that had been found. Sadly, they all related to commercial matters like sales records, contracts, guarantees and the like. There was nothing to do with John Giddings' plans for his estate. Bess was heartbroken.

Maybe this note of John's doesn't exist? Maybe George is bluffing? What if he's forged a signature on something? He must know his son's handwriting well enough to copy it?

Bess's mind was exhausted by the worry.

"Why don't you take a seat, Miss Bess? You have worn yourself out being the nursemaid, doing all this fruitless searching. You must still be in shock with the death of your 'usband. That poor little bairn you're carrying don't 'elp, neither."

Meg and Sarah tied the paper back up in the bundles and began to replace it again in the counter. Bess took herself off to the back room and paced about not knowing whether to sit or stand.

As they kneeled down, fighting to get the false base back in position, they were interrupted by the clang of the opening door once more, as it hit the small bell above. Sarah and Meg's heads popped up in unison, about to say the shop was closed, when they saw a well-dressed man at the door, holding a briefcase.

"Hello, Mr Mortimer."

"I am here to see Mrs Giddings. I think I have found something of interest."

Bess called out to the solicitor:

"Please do come through to the back, Mr Mortimer."

She hoped that the briefcase contained the all-important confirmation about her husband's wishes.

George Giddings had been stirred from his slumber by the shop bell and the shout and came downstairs to see who had visited the shop when it was supposed to be closed for the day.

He stood at the doorway to the sitting room looking at Mr Mortimer, who was now sat opposite Bess at the dining table.

The solicitor cleared his throat, then began reading, peering at the small text through his glasses.

"This is the last will and testament of me, John William Giddings of Woodborough in the county of Lincolnshire, made the twenty-first day of May in the year of our Lord one thousand eight hundred and fifty-two as follows—"

1852! That was a while ago! Well before our marriage! What if George Giddings is telling the truth, even if he lied about the whereabouts of the document!

Devastated, Bess listened as Edward Mortimer read on.

"I give and devise my hardware store, the dwelling surrounding it, now in my own occupation in Woodborough, and all my goods and chattels, to my father, George Benjamin Giddings, therefore for the purpose of providing for him in as comfortable a manner as can be.

"I desire that his sister, Anne Sarah Giddings shall be permitted to live with him for the duration of his (or her) life to take care of and maintain his clothing, cook his meals and perform domestic chores on his behalf. She will be granted a sum of four shillings a week from my estate as an income—"

Bess was horrified. Glancing over to the corner of the room, she saw George Giddings begin to smile broadly.

The conniving, unfaithful woman has finally got what she deserved. Nobody would touch her now she's pregnant with another man's child. It's the workhouse for her and her unborn bairn.

Too angry to look at his smug face any longer, she stared down at the table as Mr Mortimer paused briefly to turn the piece of paper over.

"Bess, are you listening. This next part is important?" urged the solicitor, noticing her mind had drifted far away from the matter in hand.

Bess looked earnestly at Mr Mortimer, slowly dying inside with dread.

"—Should I be unmarried on my death—"

Everyone's ears pricked up.

"Yes, this is the bit here," he said before continuing to read, "—in which case if I have a spouse, all my aforementioned assets will become the property of my wife alone."

The rapid reversal of the expressions on the faces on George Giddings and Bess could not be more pronounced. The old man had a relapse, whether real or imagined and had to be escorted upstairs by Meg at Bess's request.

"So, it seems, I am now the owner of the Giddings' Hardware Emporium and its lodgings—does it not, Mr Mortimer? How wonderful. Here, let me see you out."

Well, that's been an eventful few days. Me, a wife, then a mistress, a widow, homeowner and shopkeeper!

A grateful Bess escorted Edward to the door and made sure the sign remained on 'closed'. Next, she went to the counter, prised up the false base and took one hundred pounds from the bag, then slowly walked upstairs to see her father-in-law.

Feeling like she was intruding, Meg left the two of them alone in George's room.

An unrepentant Bess stood at the side of the bed, looking down at him, then matter-of-factly explained what would happen next.

"I think once you're well enough, which I am sure will be very soon, you should leave this property. I will give you this money as a goodwill gesture to make sure that you can set up a new life. I suggest you contact relatives and see if they will take you in. If not, you might be able to get some work in another shop, perhaps that will tide you over. Whatever happens, this is no longer your home."

She left the room, to find Meg and Sarah at the top of the landing listening to every word.

They both gave her a hug and whispered:

"You can finally be happy now, Miss. You'll have enough money to raise the child to remind you of your husband."

Bess still thought it best not to tell them the bairn was her lover's who was very much still alive. *It's time to tell Harry I am free to be with him. I can't wait!*

29

THE MASTERPLAN SINKS WITHOUT TRACE

Eager to share the latest development in the Giddings saga, Bess made her way directly to the gamekeeper's cottage. In fact, when she hit the lane, she almost broke into a run—most unbecoming for a newly widowed, and expectant woman—but she didn't care. She wanted nothing more than to see her true love; especially now she was free from her doomed marriage.

She bounced up the path and looked through the open front door, but the sight that greeted her was terrifying. *What's happened to him!* Although Harry's physical injuries might have been clearing up since the fight, left alone, the mental scars still haunted him. His mood had darkened since hearing about her pregnancy. He'd been agonising for days. The same thoughts were on repeat.

Bess wanting us to run away as 'man-and-wife' and live happily ever after is a folly. It'll be impossible. Bigamy means a life of constant secrecy and looking over our shoulders. We might get away with living-in-sin in a big city, but in a close-knit rural community where everyone knows everyone else's business, it would be out of the question. If I stay, seeing my child raised by another man will be unbearable—seeing Bess with another man will be unbearable. Besides, who would want a gamekeeper with feeble hands like these, anyway? Why are they taking so long to heal?

In his melancholic state, the future was not looking rosy for young Harry Sutherland—at all. Plus, there were other factors at play. He was slumped in a chair, the neck of an almost empty bottle of spirits gripped loosely in his right hand. The damage to his tendons after falling on the cut glass in the pub still lingered.

A shadow of his former self, he sat with his head flopping like a freshly sprung jack-in-a-box complete with a painted-on vacant stare. Muttering quietly, he berated himself for the string of poor decisions that had led events to conspire against him of late.

Bess was shocked at the state of him. The coward in her wanted to walk away, but as always, she prevailed.

She kneeled in front of him, calling out his name a few times, then waited for his rolling eyes to focus.

"What brings you here, Bess. You don't need me. Go to that husband of yours and be a happy family. Tell him the child is really his. Tell him you lied to hurt him for his attack on me. You can have a comfortable life without me. John Giddings is a far better man—"

He took the bottle and finished the last of the liquor in a sign of drunken defiance. Then he hurled it across the room, smashing it in the fireplace. A fearful Bess decided to move towards the door.

"Listen to me, Harry," she said, shaking him. "Listen."

Who does she think she is? He stared at her for a moment, then promptly passed out.

Angry but determined, Bess waited impatiently for Harry to come around from his stupor. At last, the moment came.

Frustrated with the wait, Bess blurted out:

"John Giddings is dead, Harry. I had hoped we might—"

An angry, still half-cut Harry rudely interrupted:

"—might what, Bess? Live happily ever after? Now you're free. You're better off without me. I'm no good for you. No one needs a crippled gamekeeper. Lord Hamilton has probably lost patience with me. I'll be in the workhouse myself soon. I suppose you'll inherit the shop? Keep it and find yourself a good man to help you run it. I don't belong chained to a till or a counter. I live for the wilds of the countryside. Leave me be."

She persevered.

"Harry, don't you understand. I'm free. I can be with you. We can go away like we planned when we last spoke, but without all the problems?"

As she said the words, looking at the shell of the man in front of her, she wondered if that was still what she wanted. Now the opportunity had presented itself; this wasn't how she'd imagined it would be.

"Bess! Stop! That's a fairy tale you've told yourself. I am no good for anythin'. Goodness knows who will take me on their estate now. And if you think I will live off you, you're mistaken. Please, just leave!"

Staying here is just going to anger him further. She couldn't believe what a cruel monster her beloved, caring Harry had become. In tears, she got ready to leave. *For good? Don't be silly. It's still the drink talking. He'll come around. Hopefully—.*

Back at the shop, she was distraught. She hoped it was being alone and too incapacitated to work properly that had blackened his mood, and he might have a change of heart. *Surely, he could get another job on the land? He doesn't have to be a gamekeeper? His hands are looking much healthier on each visit.*

Bess wondered if life could get any worse. *I hope not. I am at my wit's end. I am tired of being resilient. I need someone to take care of me for once.*

With her lifelong confidants and supporters Meg and Sarah by her side, within days, Bess soon felt able to face the world once more. She dusted herself off and prepared to start again, with her new life as a shopkeeper. One big problem had been solved. George Giddings had left, going to live with his younger brother, so that was something. Guilt was another matter, though. It was eating away at her.

Bess decided to pay Harry an early morning visit, hoping he would be sober this time—and calmer. Annoyed to see her trundle up the path, disobeying his instructions, he bellowed out of the window:

"I told you to keep away."

She complied with his request to avoid more arguing, thinking that he was rapidly becoming as loathsome as her dead husband. Angry thoughts of Harry Sutherland kept her awake that night. *Why couldn't he be the man he used to be? Don't our years of friendship count for something? We could be together if it wasn't for his pigheadedness.*

30

THE PHOENIX FROM THE ASHES

With her characteristic independent streak, Bess decided it was time to look to herself for answers, rather than rely on others. Things with Harry had gone from a promising start to an utter disappointment. *Why couldn't I just find a good man like Harriet had?* Her marriage to William Burridge was a success. They were happy and looking forward to the future together. *What does the future hold for me? The grinding tedium of spinsterhood?* Sensing her loneliness building, she asked Richard and Nell to visit. She felt it would cheer her spirits. Mulling over a complete overhaul of her life, all alone, was exhausting. It would be useful to sound out some options with the people she trusted most.

Over a simple lunch made by Meg, the five of them were to discuss the pregnant and widowed Bess's options. They sat in silence as Sarah served out the food.

Do I tell them it's really Harry's child? Just start, Bess, you can't stay silent when you summoned them to be with you. Get on with it.

In the end, it turned out that Nell would be the one to break the silence.

"I suppose I should tell you how my pupil-teacher training is progressing?"

Picking up a chunk of bread to dip in his soup, Richard nodded at her encouragingly.

"My progress was coming along nicely, but—"

"But?" pressed Richard.

"Jonathan Carlyle broke off our engagement. Just last week. I am not the catch I once was, apparently, now our wealth has evaporated. He ended our betrothal by leaving a note on my writing desk when I was out one day."

"I hate living there with my aunt and uncle now the marriage is no longer to take place. I feel like you must have done when you first arrived, Bess. There is a roof over your head, but it doesn't feel like home?"

Bess nodded. She had walked many miles in those shoes.

"I am looking for somewhere else, but my wages are so low, I doubt I'll find somewhere. Things have turned into a bit of a struggle. And I've realised, when

I get married, I'll have to give up teaching anyway. It all seems a bit futile."

The topic of having little choice in the quality or direction of your life was a popular one amongst their branch of the Harveys of late, it seemed.

Richard decided to share his news next.

"Uncle David has suggested I live near him. There are some nice foreman's cottages by his colliery. One or two are empty. He says if I help him manage the pit, I can have one. I fear he's only asked me out of pity. I am too old to be an apprentice and learn another trade, and I don't want to be stuck with mining until I breathe my last. It's never sat well with me as a profession. How am I supposed to get married when everything is so uncertain? It seems the luck our parents had matching Harriet has fizzled out. No one seems to want me, Nell has been ostracised, and you are a young pregnant widow, Bess. We are like a Shakespearian tragedy!"

Keen on changing the depressing subject matter, Bess had found her tongue. It was time, at last, to say what she wanted to happen in her life.

"As you know, with Mr Giddings' father now living with his brother, and Mr Mortimer has confirmed that I can take over the shop with immediate effect, I am keen to take on this store in the long term. It provides a useful service to the people of Woodborough. I have looked at the books. There seems to be a good profit to be made here. We are the only hardware store for a good few miles. Thankfully, the stack of papers we found in the hollowed-out base of the counter had lots of details for suppliers, price lists, brochures and the like, so replenishing the stock should be relatively straightforward."

"And you have the big bag of money we found, Miss Bess," smiled Meg, cheekily. "Plenty of money for stock there."

That was the easy bit. Bess now needed to make the more significant announcements.

"Of course, two people used to run this shop before me. And that is why I've asked you here—Nell—Richard."

She looked them directly in the eye with authority as she mentioned their names. It was time for 'Good Queen Bess' to hold court.

"I feel you can make a good job of running this hardware store. You have confirmed my suspicions that you are both somewhat adrift with your careers at the moment, unsure of where your future path will lead. May I suggest a wonderful opportunity could lie ahead of you here? The premises and the lodgings are paid for, so you can live here rent-free. Nell, you have said there are several drawbacks to teaching as a profession for a young woman, plus your arrangement to live with the Carlyles has broken down after the ending of your engagement."

Bess continued.

"Equally, Richard, as you mentioned, your talents do
not lie with the mining industry. I suspect you fell
into it, eager to follow in father's footsteps, but for no
other reason than that. Is it your life's dream? I think
not. Meg and Sarah can take care of you both, as you
learn the skills required to run a hardware store. The
neighbouring shopkeepers will surely help you with
any questions. We also have funds to invest in Mr
Mortimer and William our brother-in-law for advice
as and when we need it."

Bess gave a commanding look, hoping they would support her idea.

"Are you with me with this plan? I appreciate that this
is not a typical arrangement that a family might have,
but I'm sure for all of us, it will be an improvement in
our circumstances."

"But what about you, Bess? What are you doing? You
and the bairn? You've not really said," asked a curious
Meg, who had looked after the urchin since she first
arrived, and felt more like a mother to her than Mrs
Harvey ever did.

*Now's not the time to talk about my love life. Look at them.
They are stunned at the news they can live here, providing
they help with the shop. Telling them about my child with
Harry and planning to elope with him will be far too much.
That's of course if he'll have me. That's all up in the air too.
Gosh, I need a break. I am tired of my mind racing!*

"Well— I really don't know if I am honest. That's a good question. I thought I had a plan for myself—" she replied, pausing carefully to censor her innermost thoughts. "After all the turmoil of late and the strain on me and the baby, I am going to go on a week's holiday by the seaside with some of the money. The change of scene as I gently promenade in the sea air will do me good. No doubt I am the talk of the town here in Woodborough. I'm going to think about the options that I have. I shall tell you about that when I return. I need to work out what is best for the child and me."

With that, she went upstairs to collect a few of her meagre belongings and put them in her travel chest—the one she had used for boarding school. Every time she started another chapter in her life, that chest came with her.

Left to mull over the offer in private as she packed, Richard and Nell agreed to a three-month trial to run the shop, and they promised to work their fingers to the bone to make it a success. Three months would be plenty of time to see if Bess's plan had merit and if they had the aptitude to become shopkeepers. Besides, compared to their other career options, this seemed the best.

They told a delighted Bess when she asked them to help her move the trunk downstairs. Once on the ground floor, they set down the luggage and hugged each other with gratitude.

Bess said, prophetically:

> "Let us not grow weary of doing good, for in due
> season we will reap, if we do not give up."

In their hearts, they knew none of them could have em-
barked on their new chapters in their lives alone.

Thirty minutes later, a coachman pulled up outside the
Giddings Hardware Emporium and helped Bess aboard.
With a clip-clop of hooves and a clatter of wheels, Bess
disappeared out of sight, Richard, Nell, Meg and Sarah
waving her tearfully off.

31

THE CHALLENGE OF FACING THE UNKNOWN

Bess leant back against the padded wall of her coach and breathed a sigh of relief. Watching the ground below glide past her, she was comforted knowing there was finally going to be space between her and everything that had happened since her mother left her with Mr Harvey, all those years ago, on the doorstep of Walton Hall, on the outskirts of Woodborough.

" I say, driver? Would you mind if we made a short detour before we continue to the railway station? I'd love to have one final look at our old family home."

Planning to never be near it again, she felt one last look meant she might perhaps close that chapter of her life for good.

"Take this little the lane towards Hamilton House, that's the quickest way."

Bess thought of all the times she had been along that route in the years she spent as a ward of the Harveys.

The coach driver pulled up as the buttery-yellow building came into view on the left.

But Bess wasn't looking to the left. Her gaze was firmly on the gamekeeper's lodge to the right.

A stunned driver saw his young passenger suddenly clamber out of the stopped carriage, and made her way along a muddy path towards the cottage. Her dress dragged in the dirt; her pale shoes were sinking into the spongy, muddy ground.

Sensing a puzzled driver's eyes on her, she shouted:

"Just a moment, Sir. I have one last errand to run. Please wait."

Bess had no idea what would greet her at the cottage.

Would he, Harry, be roaring drunk again? The Beast of Hamilton House. Or will I meet with that kind, loving man who rescued me, tended my wounds after my cruel stepmother locked me in the boathouse? Whatever happens, I need to know either way before this week of contemplation begins.

"Harry!" She called out.

"Harry!"

There was no answer; he didn't seem to be there—or maybe he was there but drunk—unconscious somewhere. Either way, she was disappointed.

She plodded back along the muddy path and to the coach driver.

She looked up to the man sat at the front. His angry face let her know this was not part of the usual service offered.

"Could I give you a few coins in return for waiting for me for an hour or so?" smiled Bess, fishing some money out of the black velvet bag. She took what she anticipated he would earn in a week. The coach driver was suddenly very accommodating to her request.

"I'll tell the boss one of the horses had a problem. But I'll only wait an hour mind. You'll get me the sack. I have other journeys to make today."

"I'll be back soon, I promise. If not come and get me just before the hour is up? Agreed?"

The driver nodded.

She made the offer not only to respect the driver's schedule but that if it turned violent with Harry, she stood a chance of rescue. *Let's hope it doesn't turn nasty!*

She returned to the cottage, determined to thrash things out with her childhood sweetheart, one way or another. She took a seat on the edge of the bed.

Thirty minutes passed. There was no sign. Bess prepared herself for the worst.

Forty-five minutes later, she heard the crunch of footsteps breaking the stems of the foliage surrounding the cottage. *Is it the coach driver?* She looked at the clock on the mantelpiece. *If it is, he's early.*

She stealthily looked out of the window and saw Harry Sutherland, free of drink and now with just the one hand sporting a light bandage. *Was he on the mend? Could he really be back to his usual self? Please let it be true!*

She sat back down, tried to hide the mud on the hem of her dress, straightened her hair, and waited for his arrival.

So tired, and unaware of her presence, he slid off his boots; his feet were sore from walking almost fifteen miles that day. *A nice sit down, that's what I need.* He'd been checking the entire perimeter of the estate for signs of poaching, having struggled to do his rounds of late. All the mantraps were sprung ready to catch an unwary chancer trying their luck. Harry Sutherland, the loyal employee, was very much back in business.

Talking of chances, Bess chose this moment to give her sweetheart his last chance too. Keeping her cards close to her chest, she announced:

"I've come to tell you I'm leaving, Harry. That coach driver outside is waiting for me. This is the last time you'll see me and our unborn child."

The words were like a knife through his heart. He looked out of the window and saw the glossy black coach waiting with her trunk. *It's true. Think, Harry. Do you really want to lose her?* The reality of the situation punched Harry Sutherland in the stomach as hard as John Giddings had done, several weeks ago.

"I'm so sorry, Bess. And ashamed. You were only trying to help me when you came to see me recently. A horrible deep blackness surrounded me back then. Made me do some stupid things. It might have begun the moment I walked into the church and saw you marrying someone else. Then there was the fight and the worry of perhaps losing my sight in one eye. My hands were taking an age to heal."

He sat next to her, staring at the floor, humiliated.

"I was alone in this damned cottage, becoming more and more dejected. You came to see me, and my yearning to lie with you overtook my willpower. You were living in Woodborough, with another man, planning to raise my child as his own. I felt like I was trapped at the bottom of a deep dark well, Bess. It was so easy to reach for a bottle to blot it all out. Silence the voices in my head. I still love you, but you don't want a selfish simpleton like me dragging you down, do you? Fickle. Feckless. You need someone to be a good father figure and husband. You'd be like a kitten thrown in the canal in a sack, to sink without trace, with me weighing you down rather than a brick."

His voice wavered. She would soon be gone from his life forever, and it was his fault for being so thoughtless and selfish.

"I think you've said enough, Harry Sutherland. You listen to me."

He nodded.

"My fortunes have changed now. I have the shop to provide me with an income. My brother and sister have offered to run the premises. It's a three-month trial for now, but I have faith in them."

She continued nervously since Harry was not giving away any clues to his emotions.

"That frees me to live wherever I like—"

Still nothing.

"—with whom I like. And, if you were to get a job at another estate, with a bigger cottage, I could join you there. I'd be able to support myself, and the child and look after you. I won't have much money, but there would be enough to get by together. Two's plenty working in that shop. I know it's not 'proper', Harry, but when have we ever been truly 'proper'? We're two loners who for some unfathomable reason are better off together, and we are soon to be three."

She rested his hand on her belly and stared into his soul with her big eyes.

Full of remorse, he took her in his arms and apologised profusely for the upset he'd caused. He kissed the top of her head and said:

"You do realise I know I belong with you Bess, don't you?"

"Good," she said with a reassuring smile. "It's time for me to go. The coach outside is due to bring me back in a week. After our arguments last week, I planned a holiday by the seaside to have some time to myself. I had a rescue plan for the others from Walton Hall, but I didn't have one for me." she smiled. "I suppose I still don't. I trust you will have an answer for me on my return, Harry Sutherland?"

"I can do better than that Bess. Thanks to Lord Hamilton, heaven knows why, I was able to get a referral to work on another estate belonging to one of his business partners. I have secured new employment there. I had chosen it for myself when I thought I'd lost you. I am due to start the week after next, at Chawton House, in Nottinghamshire. Now I am a few years older than when I started here, I can prove I can take on more responsibility, so the gamekeeper's cottage is bigger too. Space for a child's bedroom. And I have been offered a modest pay rise. I couldn't refuse."

Bess could hardly contain her excitement.

"I shall get the coach driver to bring me back here first, in exactly one week and we can pick up where we left off—before the drink, and the darkness got to you."

Harry smiled in agreement.

With that, Bess kissed him and returned to the coach driver, and with a couple of firm cracks of his whip, the horses trotted the rest of the way up the lane.

Chawton House sounds perfect. Now, it's time for some rest.

A week later, as promised, Bess returned to Harry's cottage, bursting with joy to see him again, for such a fortuitous occasion—the start of their new life as a couple.

The next morning, they made their way to the shop. Bess went in first.

"You're back, Bess," said Richard and Nell in unison.

"Shall I help you with your luggage, Bess?"

"No need, Richard. Someone else has helped me with it."

At that moment, Harry Sutherland, now back to full health, brought in her travelling chest.

Bess's brother and sister, and the two surprised servants, listened to the news that they were a couple, and off to live on a new estate— soon to be man and wife.

"And child." Added Harry, smiling at Bess.

Meg thought back to the time she had seen Bess go to meet her beloved gamekeeper alone just before her wedding. *I was right. She was sweet on him all along. That solves that little puzzle. The urchin of Walton Hall has got her man in the end.*

Printed in Great Britain
by Amazon